"I'm intrigued, he murmured, strolling into the bedroom just as Sienna emerged from the en suite bathroom. "First you were at the church and now I find you in my bedroom. Not that I am complaining," he assured her. Far from it. Lust as hot as molten lava rushed through his veins when she ran her fingers through her hair. Was the gesture a deliberate ploy to make him notice the glossy waves that had been hidden beneath her hat in the church?

Nico had no idea what was going on, but when he flicked his gaze to the four-poster bed, his libido didn't give a damn why his incredibly sexy ex-wife was in his room.

"This is crazy," she whispered. "I did not have an ulterior motive for coming to your room." She lifted her chin and said in a firmer voice, "I don't care what you think, Nico. I'm not the besotted teenage bride who was in awe of you. I've changed."

"But this hasn't changed."

Chantelle Shaw lives on the Kent coast and thinks up her stories while walking on the beach. She has been married for over thirty years and has six children. Her love affair with reading and writing Harlequin stories began as a teenager, and her first book was published in 2006. She likes strong-willed, slightly unusual characters. Chantelle also loves gardening, walking and wine!

Books by Chantelle Shaw

Harlequin Presents

Acquired by Her Greek Boss
Hired for Romano's Pleasure
The Virgin's Sicilian Protector

Secret Heir of Billionaires

Wed for His Secret Heir

Wedlocked!

Trapped by Vialli's Vows

Bought by the Brazilian

Mistress of His Revenge
Master of Her Innocence

The Saunderson Legacy

The Secret He Must Claim
The Throne He Must Take

Visit the Author Profile page
at Harlequin.com for more titles.

Chantelle Shaw

REUNITED BY A SHOCK PREGNANCY

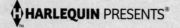

Recycling programs
for this product may
not exist in your area.

ISBN-13: 978-1-335-47823-8

Reunited by a Shock Pregnancy

First North American publication 2019

Printed in U.S.A.

REUNITED BY A SHOCK PREGNANCY

For my girls, Rosie and Lucy. So proud of the strong, independent women you have become.

xxx

CHAPTER ONE

SHE SHOULDN'T BE HERE! Not at her ex-husband's wedding.

Sienna Fisher glanced frantically around the packed church, wondering if she could escape without anyone noticing.

There was not a chance, she decided, her heart sinking. She was wedged into a pew filled with guests, and sitting next to her was the little girl she had found crying outside in the graveyard. Sienna's maternal instincts had been aroused by the child's distress and she'd taken hold of her hand and led her into the church via the vestry to find her grateful mother, who was sitting on the other side of her daughter.

The organist started playing and as the rousing notes of Handel's *Arrival of the Queen of Sheba* soared to the rafters, a ripple of interest ran through the congregation. Every head turned towards the main door to catch a first glimpse of the bride. Only Sienna stared straight ahead at the broad shoulders of Domenico De Conti, the man she had married in this very church ten years ago.

Standing with Nico was his younger brother, Daniele. Both men were tall but Nico had the advantage of a good three inches over Danny. Despite a five-year age-gap the brothers had always been close, and it was no surprise to Sienna that Nico had chosen Danny to be his best man again—just as he had done for *their* wedding.

Her breath caught in her throat when Nico turned his head. She assumed he would look towards his bride but instead his gaze was focused directly on *her*, as if some sixth sense had alerted him to her presence. From across the nave, she sensed his shock. Evidently her wide-brimmed hat did not conceal her face as well as she had hoped it would, but she hadn't planned to hang around long enough for Nico to notice her. She'd just wanted a glimpse of the man she had once been madly in love with before he had betrayed her and broken her heart.

Sienna hadn't intended to enter the church, and, earlier, she had hidden behind a tombstone when she'd seen Nico and Danny arrive. Nico must still have a passion for fast cars and had driven himself to his wedding in a sleek silver sports car. She'd watched the two men chat to the vicar for a few minutes before they had walked into the church, and she'd been about to leave when she was alerted to the sound of a child sobbing.

It was purely by accident that she was part of the congregation. Her heart fluttered in panic. She was too far away from Nico to make out the colour of his eyes that burned into her like laser beams, but she knew they were the bright blue of the sky above the moors on a cloudless summer's day. His eyes and incredible bone structure were the only features he had inherited from his English mother, but for the rest: his almost black hair that was swept back from his brow, the dark stubble shading his jaw and his olive-gold skin denoted his Italian heritage.

Ten years ago Nico had been a boyishly handsome bridegroom. Now he was in his mid-thirties, his features had honed and hardened to chiselled perfection. He was sinfully gorgeous, with a latent strength and power in his whipcord body that his elegant grey morning suit could not disguise.

Sienna snatched her gaze from Nico's, shaken by the effect he had on her after all this time. They had been divorced for eight years and she had come to the church today to prove to herself that she was over him. Her heart thudded as she waited for him to denounce her. Surely he would stop the wedding and instruct an usher to escort her from the building.

She felt her cheeks grow warm at the prospect of being humiliated in front of the population of the Yorkshire village where she had grown up. Although she hadn't recognised many locals in Much Matcham's pretty church of St Augustine's. She supposed that most of the guests at the high-society wedding were from London, or Verona where Nico's hotel business, De Conti Leisure, was based.

Her eyes were drawn involuntarily back to his dangerously attractive face and a sizzle of heat seared her body, a hunger that only Nico had ever stirred in her. Even more confusing was the fierce possessiveness that swept through her. He was *hers*, cried a voice inside her. But in a few minutes he would promise himself to another woman. Tears, hot and unexpected, stung her eyes when he finally turned his head away and looked to the front of the church while he waited for his bride.

Sienna's hands shook as she pretended to study the order of service sheet that an usher had given her. 'We're running a little late,' the usher had told her, interrupting her attempt to explain that she wasn't actually a wedding guest. 'Are you a friend of the bride or groom?'

'Groom, I suppose, but…'

'Sit here, please.' The usher had practically pushed her into a pew and now she was trapped and about to witness the marriage of her ex-husband to the vision of ethereal loveliness, wearing an exquisite wedding gown, who had joined Nico in front of the altar.

Except that it wasn't Nico. It was his brother standing next to the bride.

'In the presence of God, Father, Son and Holy

Spirit, we have come together to witness the marriage of Daniele to Victoria,' the vicar intoned.

It was Danny's wedding! A riot of emotions
stormed through Sienna. Her thoughts flew back
to the previous weekend when she had visited her
grandmother at the nursing home in York where
ninety-year-old Rose Fisher had moved to eighteen
months ago.

'Much Matcham's local newspaper is delivered to
me every week and I was surprised to read that your
husband is getting married again,' Grandma Rose
had commented over tea and scones.

Sienna's stomach had swooped and she'd set her
cup back on its saucer clumsily so that the delicate
china rattled. 'There's no reason why my *ex*-husband
shouldn't remarry,' she'd said coolly. But nothing
fooled her grandmother and Rose had given her a
sharp look. 'I imagine he needs a wife to help him
run Sethbury Hall, and…give him an heir.' Pain had
lanced through Sienna. Her inability to have a child
was something she tried not to think about, just as
she deliberately blocked out thoughts of the baby she
had lost years ago.

'Who is Nico marrying?' She'd striven to sound
uninterested as she'd taken the newspaper from
Grandma Rose and skimmed down the births, deaths
and marriages column to read the announcement
of the wedding of Miss Victoria Harington and Mr
Domenico De Conti, which would take place on the

tenth of June at St Augustine's church in Much Matcham. There had not been a picture of the couple,
and now, as Sienna watched *Danny* turn his head and
smile at his bride, she could only suppose that the
paper had muddled the De Conti brothers' names.

The rest of the wedding ceremony passed in a
blur until the vicar finally pronounced that Daniele
and Victoria were husband and wife. As the couple
walked back down the aisle and the guests spilled
from the pews to follow them out of the church, Sienna edged towards the vestry, hoping to slip away
unnoticed.

'Sienna? What are *you* doing here?'

She had almost made it to the vestry door when an
achingly familiar voice made her freeze and simulta-
neously sent molten heat flooding through her veins.
Nico's husky accent had always made her weak at
the knees. There was nothing she could do but try to
brazen it out, and she squared her shoulders before
she swung round to face him.

'Hello, Nico.' Was that breathless, sexy voice
hers? Sienna cursed silently, flushing when she saw
mockery in his piercing blue eyes. He skimmed his
gaze over her in a proprietorial manner that was to-
tally inappropriate considering their history. She felt
a sharp, almost painful tingle in her nipples, and
did not need to glance down to know that the betraying hard peaks were visible beneath her yellow
silk dress.

She had deliberately worn a summery outfit: a white hat decorated with yellow flowers, champagne-coloured stilettos and matching handbag so that people would assume she was one of the wedding guests milling around outside the church before the ceremony. The predatory gleam in Nico's eyes màde her acutely conscious of how the close-fitting dress clung to her breasts and hips and the silky material felt sensuous against her skin.

Up close he was even more devastating. A shaft of sunlight filtering in through one of the high windows danced in his night-dark hair and emphasised the hard angles and planes of his face. He smelled divine. Sienna breathed in the spicy notes of his aftershave mixed with something else that was evocatively male and uniquely Nico. An unbidden memory filled her mind, of him sprawled on the tangled sheets after they had made love, sweat beading the dark hairs on his chest, his shaft already hardening again as he pulled her down on top of him.

In the early days of their marriage they hadn't been able to keep their hands off each other and their passion had been explosive. But that was before she had lost the baby, and then sex had been dictated by fertility charts as her desire to fall pregnant again had become an obsession that had driven a wedge between her and Nico.

She was an idiot to have come here today, Sienna thought bleakly. It would have been better if she had never seen him again. Kinder to her foolish heart that still yearned for the relationship they had once had, even though her sensible head knew it had been a romantic fantasy she had built up in her imagination. But she wasn't imagining the frank awareness in Nico's eyes. She was overwhelmed by his raw sexual magnetism and dismayed by her reaction to him.

'Sienna.' The impatience in his voice pulled her mind back to the present and her embarrassing situation. 'I didn't see your name on the guest list.' He frowned. 'I'm certain Danny would have told me that he had invited you to his wedding.'

'I…um…' She could feel her face burning. 'I saw in the local paper that Danny was getting married at St Augustine's. Churches are open to the public and anyone has the right to attend a wedding taking place in a church. I wanted to give Danny and his new bride my best wishes.'

Nico's eyes narrowed. 'It's odd that you knew it was my brother's wedding. The local paper mixed up our names when they printed the forthcoming marriage announcement.'

'My grandmother told me.' Sienna crossed her fingers behind her back as she made the white lie. 'Rose keeps in touch with your grandmother and when they spoke recently, Iris told her about Danny's wedding.'

She lifted her chin and forced herself to meet Nico's speculative gaze, hoping to project an image of cool composure she did not feel. Her insides were churning, her heart was racing and there was a dull ache low in her pelvis that made her press her thighs tightly together.

'So you didn't come because you hoped to see me?' he drawled.

'Of course not. What reason could I possibly have for wanting to see you again?' She was defensive, mortified that he might guess the truth. 'Our disaster of a marriage was over a long time ago.'

'I wouldn't call it a disaster,' he murmured, taking her breath away with that mind-boggling statement. 'There were good times.' His voice lowered in a way that sent a shiver across Sienna's skin. 'Some very good times.'

'When we were in bed, you mean?' She had intended to sound sarcastic but the words emerged as a whisper. She licked her dry lips with the tip of her tongue. When had Nico moved closer so that his thigh was almost touching hers? 'A marriage needs more to sustain it than dynamite sex.'

His lips twitched and she hated that he found her amusing, but when he spoke there was no mockery in his voice, nor in the fierce gleam in his eyes. 'We were dynamite together, weren't we, *cara*?'

'Don't,' she said sharply, trying to ignore the leap her heart gave at his careless endearment. She stiffened when he lifted his hand and brushed his finger lightly down her cheek. The action was a blatant invasion of her personal space but she didn't pull away, couldn't. Her feet were glued to the floor and her gaze was trapped by his as she drowned in the cobalt-blue depths of his eyes. Everything faded and there were only the two of them standing in the church where they had once promised to love and honour each other, forsaking all others, for the rest of their lives.

Nico lowered his head so that his impossibly wicked mouth was inches from hers. 'You are even more beautiful than my memory serves me, Si-*enna*.' He rolled the syllables around his tongue, making her name sound like a caress. 'It makes me wonder why I let you go.'

The spell shattered and she jerked away from him so forcefully that her hip bone collided with the end of a pew. 'You were sleeping with your secretary.' Hurt and humiliation, those two poisonous serpents that had haunted her for years, coiled inside her. 'You didn't let me go, I chose to leave,' she snapped, her voice too loud, bouncing off the walls of the church.

'Oh, Nico, there you are,' came a softer voice. Looking past him, Sienna wished the floor would open up and swallow her when she saw Nico's grand-mother manoeuvring her wheelchair along the aisle towards them. But if Iris Mandeville had heard her angry outburst she made no comment. 'Sienna, how delightful to see you.' The elderly woman greeted her warmly. 'How is your grandmother? I haven't spoken to Rose for months.'

Sienna flushed when Nico gave her a hard stare. Clearly he was wondering how she could have known it was Danny's wedding if Iris had not told Grandma Rose.

'I am unable to visit Rose so often now that she lives in York and I have to use this wretched contraption.' Iris tapped the arm of her wheelchair. 'Rheumatoid arthritis has left me rather immobile,' she answered Sienna's unspoken question before turning her attention to her grandson.

'Domenico, you are wanted for the photographs. I can't get my wheelchair down the church steps but there is disabled access through the vestry. Sienna, my dear, would you be so kind to help me out to the car? Hobbs is bringing it round to the side of the church. Jacqueline was supposed to help me, but of course she wants to be included in the photographs.'

Sienna had noticed Nico and Danny's mother during the ceremony. Jacqueline Mandeville loved being the centre of attention and her extravagant hat festooned with ostrich feathers had made her impossible to miss. When Sienna had married Nico, her mother-in-law had worn a dramatic ivory-coloured outfit, which had outshone her store-bought wedding dress. She had been so young and unsure of herself, she remembered ruefully. Her voluminous dress had hidden her baby bump, but everyone in the church, everyone in the village, had known that she was pregnant.

She jerked her mind from the past and forced a smile for Nico's grandmother. 'Yes, of course I'll push your wheelchair out to the car.'

Footsteps sounded on the stone floor behind her. 'Nico, I've been looking everywhere for you,' a voice said tersely. 'The photographer wants to take group pictures and Victoria is going into meltdown because you'd disappeared and one of the bridesmaids says she feels sick.' Daniele De Conti stopped dead and stared. '*Sienna?* Wow! You look amazing.'

'Hello, Danny,' she murmured, taken aback by the undisguised male interest in Nico's brother's eyes. He had only been married for five minutes! But she remembered that he had always been an incorrigible flirt. Danny was a year older than her and when they were teenagers he'd asked her out a couple of times. But it had been nothing serious, and the minute she'd met Nico she'd only had eyes for him.

Against her will, her gaze was drawn to Nico, and her heart collided with her ribs when she recognised a glint of possessiveness in his eyes as well as something hotter, hungrier that sent a tremor through her. She was barely aware that Danny was speaking again.

'I must say you are the last person I expected to be here today, Sienna.'

'I just came to the church...' she began awkwardly, feeling herself blush. She tensed when Nico slid his arm around her waist.

'Sienna is here because I invited her,' he told his brother smoothly. 'I didn't reveal the name of my plus-one guest as there was a chance that Sienna wouldn't be free to travel to Yorkshire this week-end. But luckily for me she was able to come to the wedding.'

What the devil was he playing at? She was conscious that Danny and Iris were both looking at her curiously but her gaze was riveted on Nico, on his mouth as he lowered his head towards her.

He was going to kiss her! She read the message in his brilliant blue eyes and her heart did a somersault. Her common sense told her to step away from him, run, scream—maybe all three, but she had never been sensible around this man. She opened her mouth to tell Danny that she wasn't Nico's plus-one guest, no way.

'Actually that's not…' The rest of her words were smothered by Nico's mouth as he crushed her lips beneath his in a fierce kiss that made her head spin. His arm felt like a band of steel around her waist and there was blatant possession in the way he clamped his hand on her hip.

Her brain told her to pull away from him and de-mand to know what he was doing. But her body re-acted instinctively to the heat emanating from him and the bold demands of his mouth on hers. The years fell away and she was eighteen again, a girl on the cusp of womanhood, standing on a wind-swept moor and overwhelmed by the wild passion that Nico stirred in her. A tremor ran through her as she opened her mouth beneath his and kissed him back. Her body recognised his touch and desire swept fierce and hot through her veins as he deepened the kiss and her lips clung to his.

And then, as suddenly and unexpectedly as it had begun, it was over. He lifted his head and she saw a hard glitter in his eyes that sent a ripple of unease through her when she reflected on how easily, how shamelessly she had capitulated to him. Would she never learn that he was dangerous to her peace of mind? Their break-up had almost destroyed her but eventually she had grown up, moved on and established a good life for herself. She could not let a kiss from a skilled seducer who knew how to press all her buttons turn her into the doormat she had been when she was Nico De Conti's teenage bride.

He withdrew his arm from her waist and she felt as if part of her had been severed. Get a grip, she ordered herself angrily. Nico had taken an outrageous liberty when he'd kissed her and she should slap his face. At the very least, she should ask him why he had lied to his brother and grandmother about inviting her to the wedding. She was about to challenge him but he swung round and started walking towards the main door of the church.

'Photographs,' he reminded a startled-looking Danny. 'Sienna, if you wouldn't mind helping Nonna to the car? I'll see you back at the hall for the reception.'

Like hell you will. She clenched her hands by her sides as she watched him stride away. His arrogance made her seethe, but out of respect for his grandmother she swallowed her furious retort.

'Domenico is so commanding, just like his grandfather was,' Iris murmured when Sienna pushed her wheelchair into the vestry and down the ramp that led out of the church. Fortunately the chauffeur was on hand to assist the elderly lady into the car, and Sienna's muttered uncomplimentary remark about her ex-husband's bossiness went unheard.

'I'm not coming to the reception,' she told Iris. 'I don't know why Nico said he had invited me to Danny's wedding. Perhaps his plus-one guest couldn't make it.' She disliked the idea that he had decided she could stand in for his current girlfriend, whoever that might be. Nico had a high sex drive and it was inconceivable that he did not have a woman in his life.

Thankfully Iris did not refer to that kiss, but Sienna unconsciously ran her tongue over her stinging lips. The taste of Nico was still in her mouth. 'I have to drive back to London this afternoon and spend the rest of the weekend preparing for an important business meeting on Monday,' she made the excuse as she stepped back from the car.

Iris nodded. 'Rose told me that your organic skin-care company is hugely successful and you have won awards for your products. She is very proud of you.'

Sienna felt a pang of guilt thinking that she should visit her grandmother more often. She tried to get up to Yorkshire once a month, but running her own business left her little leisure time. She frowned, trying to remember when she had last met up with her friends for a drink. And as for dating, it was over a year since she had accepted a dinner invitation from a man.

Why had she allowed her social life to dwindle to practically nothing? she asked herself. She was only just twenty-nine and she had a sudden sense that life was passing her by. She loved her career and the independence it gave her but she was aware that something was missing. Love, companionship, *sex*. Where had that thought come from? Her lack of a sex life had never bothered her before today, but when Nico had kissed her it had felt as if a floodgate had opened and need had throbbed between her legs.

She was jolted from her thoughts when she realised that Iris seemed to be struggling to breathe. The elderly lady clutched her chest.

'What's wrong? Are you feeling unwell?' Sienna asked urgently.

'I'm having an angina attack,' Iris gasped. 'I thought I had put my medication in my handbag. It's a pump spray that I use under my tongue. But it's not here.' She closed her handbag that she had been rifling through. 'I must have left it in my bedroom.'

'Should I call an ambulance?'

'There's no need. I'll be fine once I have my medication. Will you come in the car with me back to the house? You can run inside and find the pump spray.'

'I'll go and fetch Nico.'

'No,' Iris said sharply. 'I don't want to cause a fuss and spoil the wedding.'

There was no time to waste arguing and Sienna ran round to the other side of the car and jumped in. The journey through the village only took a few minutes. When the chauffeur turned onto the driveway of Sethbury Hall she felt a familiar sense of awe as she stared at the imposing manor house where she had once lived with Nico. She had always felt like an imposter. The daughter of the village publican who had married above her station, some of the villagers had whispered. Cinderella had found her prince, but the fairy tale had ended in a bitter divorce.

The car came to a halt and Iris said faintly, 'You remember where my room is, Sienna? The pump spray should be on my bedside table. Please hurry.'

CHAPTER TWO

NICO LOCATED HIS grandmother in the orangery but Sienna wasn't with her. He strolled across to the open glass doors and scanned the terrace where most of the guests had congregated, but there was no sign of a yellow dress.

His jaw tightened. Inexplicably he was disappointed that his ex-wife hadn't accompanied Iris to Sethbury Hall. Frankly it was something of a surprise that Sienna had disobeyed him. When they'd been married she had always been eager to please him, especially in bed. Sometimes her puppy-like devotion had irritated him but she had been very young; a teenage bride, sweetly shy and biddable.

He frowned, remembering her accusation on the day she had walked out of their marriage that he had taken her for granted. With hindsight perhaps he had, he thought uncomfortably. *Dio*, but he had been young himself, with a weight of duty and responsibility on his shoulders. Sienna had been another of his responsibilities. Pregnant with his child and terrified of her abusive father. Nico had done the only thing he could do and offered to marry her.

He cursed beneath his breath. The last thing he wanted was a trip down memory lane. When he'd spotted Sienna in the church earlier he had thought at first that he must have imagined her. Standing in front of the altar with his brother had evoked memories of his own wedding ten years earlier, when Danny had been his best man.

Nico remembered the sense of panic he'd felt on his wedding day, of being trapped. He'd looked over his shoulder towards the door, wondering if he could make a run for it. But at that moment Sienna had walked into the church. She had looked exquisite in her bridal gown, with her long hair streaming down her back. She'd held a bouquet of cream roses over her stomach and looked as nervous as he felt.

He'd accepted that he couldn't abandon her and his baby, and as he'd watched her walk towards him, he had been impatient for their wedding day to be over so that he could take her to bed. Their passion was white-hot and when he was buried deep inside her he did not care that he was marrying her out of duty. She was his exclusively and she was carrying his child. At least that was what he had believed then.

Nico jerked his mind away from the past and declined the glass of sherry a waiter offered him.

He could do with a drink but his preferred poison was oak-barrel-aged cognac. As he strode up the sweeping staircase to his private suite of rooms, he told himself that he could take a short break from his best-man duties. Danny and his elegant bride were mingling with their guests while canapés were served on the terrace.

Entering his sitting room, he went straight to the bar and poured himself a drink. The cognac was smooth and mellow with a pleasant heat at the back of his throat. He looked across the room, puzzled that his bedroom door was open. He was sure it had been shut when he'd left the suite earlier. His heart kicked in his chest when he saw a white hat decorated with yellow flowers on the bed.

'I'm intrigued, *cara*,' he murmured, strolling into the bedroom just as Sienna emerged from the en-suite bathroom. 'First you were at the church and now I find you in my bedroom. Not that I am complaining,' he assured her. Far from it. Lust as hot as molten lava rushed through his veins when she ran her fingers through her hair. Was the gesture a deliberate ploy to make him notice the glossy waves that had been hidden beneath her hat in the church?

Her hair was the same shade of dark red as a vintage burgundy wine and he knew the colour was entirely natural. When she was younger her hair had been waist-length, but now it fell to just past her shoulders with layers framing her face and drawing attention to her peaches-and-cream skin and wide grey eyes.

'Your bedroom?' Sienna frowned. 'I thought your grandparents occupied the master suite?'

'They did when my grandfather was alive. But my grandmother has become less mobile in the last few years and when she moved into the new annexe on the ground floor I had these rooms refurbished.'

'That would explain why I can't find her medicine. Iris gave me the impression that she still used the same rooms as she did when I lived at Sethbury Hall. I expect she was confused. She asked me to fetch her angina pump spray, but I couldn't find it on the bedside table and I've been looking for it in the bathroom cupboards.'

'I don't understand why Nonna asked you.'

'She was having an angina attack.' Impatience flashed in Sienna's eyes. 'Don't just stand there. Your grandmother looked in a bad way and she needs her medication. How do I get to the annexe?' She went to step past him and stiffened when he caught hold of her arm.

'I meant why did she send you to get her medicine rather than one of the household staff who know where her rooms are?' Nico's eyes narrowed. 'Iris seemed perfectly well when I saw her a few minutes ago. She does suffer from angina but she takes tablets to control it. As far as I am aware she hasn't had an attack since she was diagnosed with the condition and she carries a pump spray merely as a precaution.'

'Well, maybe she forgot to take her tablet and that's why she had an angina attack.' Sienna threw her hands in the air. 'Don't you believe me? Why would I make something like that up?'

'To give you an excuse to visit my bedroom?' Nico had no idea what was going on but when he flicked his gaze to the four-poster bed, his libido didn't give a damn *why* his incredibly sexy ex-wife was in his room.

She whirled away from him and he noted how her silky dress clung to the rounded curves of her pert derriere. Fire licked through his veins and burned even hotter when she faced him and put her hands on her hips, causing her dress to pull tight across her breasts. Despite her slender build, Sienna had always been full up top, and Nico was definitely a breast man.

'That's right.' Her sarcastic tone forced his gaze up to her face and he was fascinated by the gleam of temper in her eyes. The girl he'd married had been timid and amenable and would not have dreamed of disagreeing with him, let alone glare at him as if she was itching for a fight. 'I was desperate to be alone with you so I invented the story that your grandmother had sent me to find her medication.' Sienna gave him a withering look. 'Your ego must be enormous if you think I was so blown away when you kissed me in the church that I want you to do it again.'

His ego wasn't the only thing that was enormous, Nico silently derided himself, conscious that his arousal was uncomfortably hard beneath his suit trousers. As for that kiss. Of course it shouldn't have happened. But he had seen the lascivious look in his brother's eyes when Danny had stared at Sienna, and he'd been overwhelmed by a fierce possessiveness, a need to claim her in front of Danny. Especially Danny.

That wasn't the only reason he had kissed her though. There had been something deeply primitive about his compelling need to put his mouth on Sienna's. It had been the same the first time he'd met her ten years ago. He had taken one look at her and known that he had to have her. He'd kissed her within the hour and slept with her three days later.

He knew every gorgeous dip and curve of her body; the little mole on her inner thigh that he'd always kissed before spreading her legs wide so that he could flick his tongue over the tight nub of her femininity until she writhed and begged him to possess her. Not that he'd needed any persuasion. Sex with Sienna had been wilder and hotter than with any other woman—a theory Nico had put to the test many times since his divorce.

He'd told himself that it couldn't have been as good as he remembered. But when he had kissed her in the church a little while ago, their chemistry had been combustible. The soft gasp she'd made as she'd parted her lips beneath his had decimated his self-control and for a few moments he had forgotten that they had an audience of his brother and grandmother.

Now though they were alone, and as he watched Sienna's tongue dart out and slide over her slightly swollen lower lip a carnal hunger tore through Nico. 'Of course you want me to kiss you again, *cara*,' he drawled. 'I can read the signs.' He lifted his hand to the front of her dress and traced the outline of one pointed nipple, wildfire coursing through him when she drew an audible breath. But she made no attempt to move away and her pupils had dilated so that her eyes were inky pools edged with silvery grey.

'This is crazy,' she whispered. 'I did not have an ulterior motive for coming to your room. I wasn't even aware that this is your room.' She lifted her chin and said in a firmer voice, 'I don't care what you think, Nico. I'm not the besotted teenage bride who was in awe of you. I've changed.'

'But this hasn't changed,' he said roughly, threading his fingers into her hair so that he could tug her even closer and angling her head. Her breasts rose and fell jerkily and her lips parted in readiness for him to claim her mouth. The sexual chemistry between them was tangible and his nostrils flared as he dragged oxygen into his lungs. But as he lowered his face to hers, she put her hand on his chest to stop him.

'What about your grandmother?' Sienna drew a shuddering breath, as if she was struggling for control as much as he was. 'She needs her angina medicine.'

'Like I said, I saw Iris just before I came upstairs. She was on her second glass of sherry and regaling the new vicar with lurid tales of her youth.' Nico exhaled heavily, aware of the dull throb of unfulfilled lust in his groin. 'But regrettably this will have to wait until later. We need to get down to the marquee in the garden for the wedding dinner, and I have various duties to perform as best man.'

He dropped his hands down to his sides but could not bring himself to move away from her. His senses were inflamed by her perfume and the sharp, sweet scent of desire—hers, his—was thick in the air.

She shook her head and walked over to the bed to pick up her hat. 'There won't be a "later", Nico. If I hadn't gone to the church we would never have met again.' She flashed him a cool smile, but something like sadness chased across her face and her grey eyes were as haunting and mysterious as the mist that sometimes came down over the moors. 'We have led separate lives for eight years. We're strangers, and I'm not going to sit through your brother's wedding reception and pretend that we are friends.'

Sienna disappeared through the door with a swirl

of yellow silk, leaving Nico faintly stunned when he realised that she was leaving him—again.

A memory flashed into his mind of when he had watched her walk out of the gates of Sethbury Hall eight years ago. She had carried a small suitcase containing the few chain-store clothes that were all she'd owned when she had married him. He had found all the designer dresses that he'd bought her hanging in the wardrobe, and she had also left behind the jewellery he'd given her, including her wedding ring.

As he'd watched her slender figure march down the driveway, her back ramrod straight, he had told himself he was glad she was leaving. *Lying bitch.* Her accusation that he had been unfaithful was all the more galling because he knew the truth about her. She was the cheat, the one who had kept secrets. *Dio*, he had trusted her, but after what his brother had told him, Nico had vowed that he would never again believe a word Sienna said.

His jaw clenched. He had never revealed to Sienna that he knew she had slept with his brother first, before him. Danny had admitted it when Nico had confided two years after his wedding that the marriage was in trouble. When Sienna had suffered a late miscarriage she had been advised to wait a few months before trying to conceive again. Nico hadn't told Danny or anyone else that after he and Sienna had tried unsuccessfully for a year to have another baby, he had done a home test, which showed he had a low sperm count.

Danny's confession had eaten away at Nico, and the suspicion that Sienna had been pregnant with his brother's child when he'd married her had festered like something rank and rotten in his soul. Sienna's accusation that he was having an affair with his PA had been the final straw. Her hypocrisy had infuriated him and divorce had been a way out of a marriage based on lies. He had set her free so that she could meet someone else who would give her a child—which he was unable to do.

He pulled his mind away from the past when he heard the click of her heels on the marble stairs and pictured her in her sexy, yellow silk dress. Ten years ago she had been a pretty teenage bride with no idea of her potential to be a stunning beauty in the future. The grown-up Sienna had exceeded all his expectations, he brooded. She was a ravishing, sensual siren and ever since he had caught sight of her in the church, desire had pulsed hot and urgent in his blood.

The sensible thing to do would be to let her walk out of his life as he had done once before. But he had never been able to forget her, and seeing her again had evoked an unexpected sense of regret that he had lost her. At the very least, he was curious to know why she had turned up in Much Matcham having read in the paper that he was getting married. Her excuse that Iris had told her grandmother Rose it was Danny's wedding was patently another lie.

Immediately after the divorce he had hated her, but now he was merely indifferent to Sienna's wiles, Nico assured himself. He grimaced as the ache in his groin reminded him that his body was not as un-involved as he'd like. But he wasn't a young man at the mercy of his hormones any more. He was older, hopefully wiser, and he had learned not to mistake lust for a deeper emotion. Undoubtedly he could han-dle his inconvenient attraction to his ex-wife.

'Nonna will be disappointed if you leave,' he called after her as he strode onto the landing and leaned over the banister rail. 'Especially as she clearly went to some lengths to make sure you came back to the house for the reception.'

Sienna paused on her way down the stairs and looked up at him. 'Emotional blackmail won't work with me. You allowed Iris to think there is some-thing going on between us but you'll have to tell her the truth.'

'Oh, I'm all for the truth, *cara*,' he murmured, walking swiftly down the stairs to join her on the half-landing. 'And the truth is we both still feel the wildfire attraction that burned between us a decade ago.' He felt a tremor run through her and saw hunger in her eyes before her lashes swept down and con-cealed her thoughts. Triumph surged through Nico, threatening the self-control he had been so confident would not waver.

'I had only left school a month before we met. What chance did I stand?' she demanded in a bitter voice. 'You were six years older than me and already worldly and experienced. In contrast I was painfully innocent but you soon changed that, didn't you, Nico? You were used to having whatever you wanted and it was my misfortune that you decided you wanted me.'

Misfortune? He had married her, hadn't he? He gritted his teeth. 'I don't remember hearing you complain, *cara*. But I do remember the moans you made when I kissed your breasts. *Please*, Nico, take me now,' he mocked, his satisfaction mixed with a stab of shame when fiery colour winged along her high cheekbones and hurt flashed in her eyes.

'You always were an arrogant bastard.' She pushed her hair back over her shoulders and he inhaled the scent of vanilla. Her foot was poised over the lower stair. 'This is a pointless conversation. No good ever comes from digging up the past. Goodbye, Nico.'

'Stay.' The word burst from him, harsher than he'd intended, but then he hadn't intended to plead with her. She stared at him, looking as shocked as he felt. She was so beautiful. He could look at her for ever and never grow tired of her delicate features. That sexy mouth of hers was a little too wide and all the more perfect for it, and her eyes were the colour of storm clouds. 'Please,' he said roughly.

She swallowed and the convulsive movement of her throat betrayed emotions that he sensed she was desperate to hide. 'I...' She did that flippy thing with her hair again, running her fingers through the layers and making him want to touch the silken strands of rich burgundy. 'Why do you want me to stay for the reception?' she asked huskily.

He shrugged to hide the fact that he was asking himself the same question. 'You said you've changed in the years since we were divorced and so have I. We are not the people we were then, but the attraction we both feel is as strong as when we first met.'

Her tongue darted across her lips. 'I don't know what you want,' she said in a low tone.

What he wanted was to whisk her back to his bedroom so that they could spend the rest of the afternoon in bed. And if she carried on looking at him with eyes that had turned smoky and held a gleam of sensual promise, he wouldn't be responsible for his actions. 'I'd like to get to know the grown-up Sienna Fisher,' Nico told her, startled to discover it was the truth.

Sienna looked around the huge marquee, which was decorated with extravagant floral displays, and sighed when Nico's grandmother gave her a friendly wave from across the room.

'My angina pump spray was in my handbag all the time. I don't know how I missed it,' she'd explained when Sienna had asked before they sat down to dinner if she was feeling better. 'I'm glad you decided to stay for the reception after all. It's good to see you and Nico getting on so well,' Iris had added pointedly.

She must be mad to have agreed to stay, Sienna thought. If Iris told Grandma Rose that she had returned to Sethbury Hall as Nico's guest, she would have some explaining to do. Nico had said that four hundred guests had been invited to the wedding. There was no top table and everyone, including the bride and groom, had sat at individual tables when the five-course meal was served by an army of white-jacketed waiters.

The food had looked exquisite but she'd been so conscious of Nico sitting beside her that she had barely tasted what she was eating. Now that the meal was over and the toasts and speeches were finished, the band had started playing and people were already on the dance floor.

Nico was talking to one of his relatives sitting on the other side of him and Sienna studied him covertly from beneath her lashes while she sipped her champagne. It was unfair that he was so indecently sexy, she brooded. His mother had been regarded as one of the great beauties of her generation. Like his grandfather before him, Nico's patrician features were an indication of an aristocratic lineage that could be traced back centuries to when English knights and barons had forced King John to sign the Magna Carta.

Jacqueline Mandeville's marriage to a handsome Italian playboy Franco De Conti, whose family's enormous fortune had derived from their exclusive hotel chain, had produced an heir and a spare, Danny had once joked to Sienna. They had been at Sethbury Hall where Nico had organised a tennis tournament with a group of friends. Sienna had been startled by the bitterness in Danny's voice. She'd told herself she must have imagined that he was jealous of his older sibling. But now, as she looked across the table and saw Danny staring at Nico with an odd expression on his face, she remembered that day all those years ago.

Nico had beaten Danny in a tennis match and Danny had stormed off the court. Later, he'd laughed and told her it was just brotherly rivalry. 'Nico wins everything, including my girlfriend,' he'd said. It wasn't strictly true. She had gone out with Danny a couple of times, but when he had tried to kiss her she'd explained that she just wanted them to be friends. Nico had arrived at Sethbury soon after and she had fallen instantly in love with him.

Sienna's mind jolted back to the present when Danny leaned across the table. 'When did you get back with my brother? I'm surprised Nico didn't mention that he was seeing you again.'

It was on the tip of her tongue to explain that she hadn't had any contact with Nico since their divorce. But there had been faint suspicion in Danny's voice, and bizarrely she wanted to protect Nico from embarrassment so she said lightly, 'Oh, we bumped into each other in London recently and he invited me to the wedding. Nico knew that you and I had been friends, and I was pleased to have the chance to wish you and your new bride a happy marriage.'

'Come and dance with me for old times' sake.' Danny stood up and walked around the table.

Sienna hesitated, unable to explain to herself why she felt reluctant to take his hand. 'I expect you want to dance with your wife.'

'Victoria is dancing with her father.' Danny tugged her out of her chair and led her over to the dance floor. He kept hold of her hand and slid his other arm around her waist. 'We were good friends when we were younger, weren't we? Do you remember when a group of us hired a river boat for the day in York and you fell in?'

'You pushed me in.'

'Ah, but I jumped in and rescued you, didn't I?' Danny went on to recount other stories from their youth, and Sienna was soon laughing at the memories. She had got to know Danny when he had been a regular at her father's pub where she'd served behind the bar most evenings and weekends, saving up to go to university. Not that her father had paid her much for all the hours she'd worked, but at least while he was being obnoxious to her he had left her mother alone.

Danny De Conti and his public school friends had seemed glamorous and exciting compared to the local boys from the village.

'Danny's not bad looking, but his older brother is drop-dead gorgeous,' the other barmaid, Becky, had told Sienna. 'Domenico spends much of his time in Italy, but my mum is a cook up at the hall and she heard that he's coming home next week. By the way, Lady Mandeville is looking for a part-time cleaner and Mum says she'll put your name forward if you like.'

Which was how, ten years ago, Sienna had been mopping the kitchen floor at Sethbury Hall when Nico had walked in, his riding boots leaving footprints where she had just cleaned. *'Mi dispiace,'* he'd murmured with barely a glance at her. But then he'd stopped and turned to stare at her, the faint frown between his eyebrows not marring the masculine beauty of his face. 'Who are you?'

She had been struck dumb; dazzled by the handsome, bronzed god who had materialised in front of her and could not possibly be real. She'd blinked but he had still been there, tall and strong-looking, his exotic appearance emphasised by his golden skin and unexpected brilliant blue eyes. As she'd stared back at him, a slow smile had lifted the corners of his gorgeous mouth and her heart had raced.

'Perhaps you are not real and that's why you don't have a name,' he'd teased. 'But if you are real your feet must be wet.'

Confused, she'd glanced down and discovered that the mop was dripping water over her trainers. 'I'm Sienna,' she'd blurted out, mortified when he'd run his eyes over her faded jeans and tee shirt. All her clothes had been years old but she hadn't had money to buy new, fashionable stuff like the other girls she'd known at school. Her tee shirt had been too tight, and because it had been a hot day she hadn't bothered to wear a bra.

To her horror she had felt her nipples harden, but when she'd hurriedly crossed her arms in front of her she had seen a gleam in Nico's eyes that had sent a delicious shiver through her. It had been the first time in her life that she'd felt desire, and in that instant she had become aware of her femininity.

'My name is Domenico, but my friends call me Nico,' he'd told her.

'I know, sir.' She'd suddenly remembered her lowly position and his exalted one. One day he would inherit Sethbury Hall and the title of Viscount Mandeville when his grandfather died.

He had laughed. 'I very much hope you will call me Nico, Si-*enna*.' Even the way he'd said her name had been sexy. 'You can't have wet feet for the rest of the day. Take off your shoes and we'll sit in the garden while they dry. You can tell me why a girl as beautiful as you is working here.'

She had been seduced by Nico's easy charm and his self-assurance that even back then had sat lightly on his broad shoulders. He had kissed her for the first time that same afternoon while they were sitting in the shade of a lilac tree covered with heavenly scented purple spires. Later she had walked home on air and even her father's drunken bad temper couldn't burst her bubble. She'd been in love with a handsome prince who she'd been sure would make all her dreams come true.

Right now, Nico looked as dangerous as the wicked wolf beloved of so many fairy tales. Time shifted to the present and Sienna found herself looking into the glittering gaze of her ex-husband. He was moving purposefully across the dance floor towards her, accompanied by the new Mrs De Conti.

'Let's swap. I don't want to be accused of monopolising your delightful bride,' he said to Danny, skilfully executing the change of partners before Sienna had time to object.

He swept her across the dance floor so fast that her head spun and her feet barely touched the floor. When she tried to ease away from him, he clamped his arm around her waist and pulled her towards him so that her breasts were crushed against his chest.

'What are you doing?' she muttered, struggling

to speak with her face pressed against his shirt front. She could see the shadow of his dark chest hairs beneath the fine white silk. The heat of his body was melting her insides.

'I could ask you the same question,' he said in a terse voice, and when she glanced up at his face she realised that he was furious. 'Did you come to Danny's wedding to cause trouble?'

She was mystified. 'What do you mean by trouble? What have I done?'

'Did you give any thought to Danny's new bride while you were flirting with him in front of the wedding guests?'

'I was not flirting...'

'You were all over him like a rash. *Dio*, you've got every male in the marquee panting over you. Why embarrass Victoria like that? Was it to prove that you can have any man you want, including my ass of a brother?'

Sienna sucked in a sharp breath, her temper rising to meet Nico's. 'You asked me to come to the reception,' she snapped. 'It's ridiculous to make me out as some sort of man-eater. No one here is interested in me.'

'I don't believe you are unaware of the effect you have on men.'

'I only have an effect on you.' The words spilled from her mouth before she realised what she had said.

Nico tensed and stared at her, and the hunger in

his eyes both excited and appalled her. He was her ex-husband and whatever there had been between them had died a long time ago, she reminded herself. So why did he make her feel dizzy and disconnected from reality?

She was barely aware of the other people on the dance floor. There was just Nico filling her vision and swamping her senses. He was even more dangerously handsome and charismatic than her memory of him but she was determined not to fall under his spell again.

CHAPTER THREE

SIENNA ATTEMPTED TO wrench herself out of Nico's arms and glared at him when he tightened his hold on her waist. 'I don't want to dance with you,' she told him, her fury mixed with panic that she could not control her response to him. She was tempted to dig one of her stiletto heels into his foot. 'You can't make me.'

'Do you want to put that to the test?' He laughed softly at her fulminating look. 'You did not have such a fiery temper when you were my wife.'

'At eighteen I was too in awe of you to say boo to a goose. But I grew up and I'm no longer the girl who worshipped the ground you walked on.'

'You've certainly changed. You are more confident and assertive, and very sexy, *cara*.' The unholy gleam in his eyes was part teasing and part male admiration that sent another sizzle of heat through Sienna. Nico dropped his hands from her waist and perversely she wished he was still holding her.

They had reached the door of the marquee, and

when she followed him outside she took a deep breath to steady her racing pulse. In midsummer the days were long, and although it was past nine o'clock, darkness was only just falling, turning the sky a soft purple hue. The air was warm and sultry, filled with the mingled scents of roses and lavender that grew in wide beds in the garden. In the distance there was an ominous rumble of thunder.

'I should go.' As she spoke, Sienna checked her watch. She would have to walk back to the village where she had left her car, and it would be completely dark when she drove across the moors to pick up the main road that led to the motorway.

'Come up to the house for a drink.' Nico's voice was casual, but when she glanced at him, something about his intent expression made her heart miss a beat.

'I can't,' she said quickly before she gave in to the temptation to spend another hour with him. It was unlikely she would ever see him again after tonight and she resented the little pang her heart gave. She was *so* over him, she reminded herself sternly. 'I had a glass of champagne when we toasted the bride and groom and I'll be over the limit to drive if I have any more alcohol. Besides, it's a good five-hour trip back to London.'

He frowned. 'You can't make that long journey tonight. Why didn't you book a hotel room?'

She shrugged, not wanting to admit that she'd

made a spur-of-the-moment decision that morning to drive to Much Matcham because she'd mistakenly believed that he was getting married and she had been curious about his choice of bride. 'No rooms were available at The George, or at any of the local B & Bs. I suppose they were all booked by the wedding guests. If I'm tired on the way home, I'll stop at a motorway services hotel.'

'You can spend the night here at Sethbury Hall.' Nico gave her a speculative look when she stared at him. 'Why not?'

'I can think of several reasons why it would be a terrible idea for me to spend the night with you.'

'As a matter of fact I was going to suggest that you sleep in one of the guest rooms,' he drawled. The amusement in his voice caused a hot stain of embarrassment to flare on Sienna's cheeks and she was furious with herself for jumping to the wrong conclusion. 'To satisfy my curiosity, why would it be a terrible idea for us to sleep together? We are attracted to each other and we're both consenting adults.'

'You've got to be kidding.' She shook her head and tried to dismiss the erotic images in her mind of Nico making love to her on his huge four-poster bed.

The gleam in his eyes made her wonder if he could read her thoughts. 'What are you afraid of?' he asked softly.

That you will break my heart for a second time.

'I'm not afraid of anything,' she snapped. 'I simply think it's a bad idea.' She hated that he tied her in knots and without another word she swung round and started to walk along the gravel path that wound around the side of the house. But she had only taken a few steps when a thunderclap shattered the still air. The noise was as loud as an explosion and Sienna jumped when a bolt of lightning zigzagged like a white scar through the sky that had turned black as the storm clouds mustered. And then the rain fell; big, hard raindrops that stung her bare shoulders and arms.

In seconds it was a deluge. Nico grabbed her hand. 'Come on,' he shouted above the crash of thunder. Half-blinded by the torrential rain, she clung to his hand as they raced up the stone steps and across the terrace. Nico opened the French doors and pulled her behind him into the drawing room. Sienna barely noticed her surroundings. She was soaked to the skin and her dress clung to her body. Following Nico's gaze, she glanced down and saw that her nipples were jutting provocatively through the wet silk.

He had closed the glass doors and the noise of the thunderstorm outside was muted. But inside the room a different storm raged. The sexual tension sparked between them and Sienna's skin prickled; every one of her nerve-endings acutely aware of him.

Nico took off his jacket and threw it carelessly over the back of a chair. He shoved a hand through his wet hair and prowled across the room towards her, as predatory as a sleek and very dangerous jungle cat. He stood in front of her, so close that the flames of desire in his eyes scorched her and she could not repress the shiver of anticipation that ran through her.

'Are you cold?' His eyes were fixed on her breasts and Sienna lost the battle with herself.

'I'm burning up,' she admitted in a husky voice she did not recognise as her own. Maybe she was crazy. All right, she was definitely crazy, but she could not make herself step away from Nico. She had wanted him from the moment she'd seen him in the church today. But she was no longer a shy eighteen-year-old, she was a confident woman who knew her own mind and was in every way his equal.

Although Sienna was wearing four-inch heels Nico towered over her. She watched his head descend and impatience swept through her. Pushing herself up onto her toes, she grabbed hold of his tie and pulled his mouth down onto hers. Just like when they had been in the church, the kiss exploded between them as their mouths fused together. He wrapped one arm around her waist and threaded the fingers of his other hand through her hair, cupping her nape and tugging her head back to allow him to plunder her lips with the mastery that was an integral part of Nico De Conti.

Sienna couldn't resist him. She had never been able to, she acknowledged. He was a sorcerer and when she was in his arms she was enchanted by his sensual magic. His kiss stole her sanity as he increased the pressure of his lips on hers and pushed his tongue into her mouth to explore her with mind-blowing eroticism.

She had missed him so much. Memories she'd tried to suppress for years burst into her mind like fireworks, silver and gold, shimmering and incandescent. The past merged with the present as she pictured them naked, their limbs entwined, his hands sliding over her body just as they were doing now. He eased away from her a fraction so that he could spread his fingers over her breasts and caress them through the silk of her dress. The warmth of his palms was intoxicating but it wasn't enough, not nearly enough.

His jacket had taken the brunt of the rain when they had been caught in the storm, but his shirt front was damp beneath Sienna's hands as she ran them over his chest. She could feel the heat of his body through the fine material and she tugged at the buttons, eager to touch his bare skin. Pulling his shirt tails from the waistband of his trousers, she gave a soft sigh as she spread the edges of the shirt wide and skimmed her fingertips over his bronzed, satin skin overlaid with whorls of silky black hair.

His hands were busy too, sliding up to tug the straps of her dress down her arms. 'There's a zip,' she muttered against his mouth when he broke the kiss so that they could both snatch a breath. He gave a grunt and claimed her lips again, hot and hungry, seeking a response she had no thought to deny him.

She lifted her hands to his shoulders and felt him slide her zip down the length of her spine. He peeled her dress from her breasts and made a rough sound in his throat when he discovered that she was braless. He dragged his thumb pads over her taut nipples, making her gasp and shudder as sensation arced down her body to meet the ache between her legs.

'You are exquisite,' Nico said hoarsely, a hard glitter in his eyes as he stared at her firm breasts, each adorned with a dusky pink nipple standing erect. *'Perfetto.'* Dull colour streaked along his sharp cheekbones and his features hardened, giving him a feral appearance that sent another shiver through Sienna.

'Let me warm you.' His voice was like rough velvet. 'Hold on tight, *cara.*' He scooped her off her feet, one arm around her waist and the other beneath her knees. She wound her arms around his neck and pressed her face against his throat, her tongue darting out to lick the faint saltiness of his skin. He tasted divine and, driven by an elemental need that only this man had ever evoked in her, she gently bit his neck.

'Dio,' he growled, his arms flexing around her as he strode out of the drawing room and across the hall. 'Wait until we are upstairs and then you can bite me all you like. But be warned that I bite back.'

He carried her up the sweeping staircase as if she weighed nothing. On the landing, he paused and sought her gaze with his bright blue eyes that burned down to her soul. 'My bedroom is along the corridor on the right, and to the left are the guest rooms. Your choice.' His tone was as blank as the expression on his far too handsome face.

For a moment Sienna wished he had made the decision for her and simply carried her to his room. That way she could absolve herself of the guilt that she was shamefully weak where he was concerned. But she wasn't the overawed girl who had married him, she reminded herself. Since their divorce she had taken control of her life and she was entirely capable of making her own decisions. She wanted everything that Nico could give her. For this one night only. A chance to come to terms with the past so that she could evict him from her mind and her heart once and for all.

'Right,' she said huskily, ignoring the voice in her head advising her to run as far and as fast from him as she could. He did not ask again, he simply turned and strode down the corridor, shouldered the door into his private suite and carried her through to his bedroom. Closing the door, he set her down on her feet and pulled her into his arms, his mouth seeking and finding hers in a kiss that was hotter and more urgent than anything that had gone before.

The top of her dress was bunched around her

waist. Nico tugged the rain-soaked silk over her hips and the dress slithered to the floor, leaving her in just a pair of tiny knickers that were wet from her arousal. His hands were everywhere on her body, sliding down her back and shaping the curves of her bottom before he pushed one hand between her legs and cupped her sex through her damp panties.

She arched her hips towards him and he muttered something in Italian as he shoved her up against the door, his mouth still fused with hers. He kissed her until she was dizzy with desire, until nothing existed but Nico's lips on her lips, her throat and then, *at last*, on her breasts as he sucked on one hard nipple and then the other.

Sienna gave a guttural cry; need pulsing through her as Nico tormented the sensitive peaks with his tongue. She skimmed her hands over his chest and flat abdomen, following the arrowing of dark hair that disappeared beneath his waistband. Hesitating for a second, she moved her hand lower and traced the hard outline of his erection straining beneath his trousers. His breath rasped in his throat, and when she lifted her eyes to his, the burning heat of his gaze added fuel to the fire inside her.

She fumbled with his zip, her knuckles scraping across his burgeoning arousal. Nico swore and pushed her hand away, yanking the zip down so that he could free himself from the constraint of his trousers and silk boxers.

Dear Lord, he was huge. Not that she had any personal experience of other men to compare him with, Sienna acknowledged. There had only ever been Nico. And it had been so long since she had felt him inside her. Molten heat pooled low in her pelvis at the thought of what she wanted him to do.

'I need you now.' She didn't realise she had spoken aloud until he made a choked sound, halfway between a laugh and a groan.

'It's the same for me, *cara*. I can't wait.' He slid his hand down her body, pushed aside the scrap of lace between her legs and eased a finger into her wet heat. She almost went up in flames. The sensation of him swirling his finger inside her and gently stretching her, before he pushed a second digit into her opening, made her gasp and tense as the first ripples of an orgasm threatened to shatter the remnants of her control.

But she wanted more, and when she felt Nico's rock-hard erection press between her thighs, her insides turned to liquid. He tugged her knickers down and she stepped out of them. 'Wrap your legs around me,' he muttered, his hands cupping her bottom cheeks as he lifted her off her feet. Sienna obeyed him mindlessly, compelled by a primal urge to take him inside her and let him possess her utterly.

She hooked her legs around his hips and somehow managed to kick off her shoes. And then he simply drove into her with a powerful thrust that made her gasp as she discovered just how hard he was, how thick, filling her inch by mind-blowing inch.

'*Dio*, you're so tight,' he said unsteadily. 'Am I hurting you? Do you want me to stop?'

'No…and no,' she whispered. It was difficult to speak past the lump in her throat. She was unprepared for the emotions that stormed through her. She felt as if she had come home. 'I just need a moment.'

She felt him start to withdraw and tightened her legs around his waist while she dug her fingers into his shoulders, pressing her breasts against his chest. His chest hair felt abrasive rubbing across her sensitive nipples, creating a delicious friction that evoked a coiling sensation low in her pelvis. 'Don't stop,' she said fiercely.

He must have sensed her urgency and the ragged groan he gave told her he shared it. Gripping her bottom cheeks tighter, he pushed her up against the door and thrust deep into her, withdrew a little way and repeated the action over and over. It was wild and frantic as he ground his hips against hers, the harsh sound of his breaths mingling with her gasps and moans. She wondered if her spine would be bruised from where Nico was holding her up against the solid wooden door, but right now there was just pleasure building inside her, intensifying with each devastating thrust as he took her higher.

His mouth captured hers again in a sensual and unexpectedly tender kiss that was nearly her undoing. 'Nico…' She gasped his name, too overwhelmed to care about the pleading note in her voice.

'I know, *cara*.' He quickened his pace and drove into her faster, harder, taking her to the edge of heaven. It was too much. He had always been too much. 'Angel, I'm going to…' His voice rasped against her throat. And then he slipped his hand between their joined bodies and flicked his thumb over the ultra-sensitive tip of her clitoris. The pleasure was so intense that Sienna shattered. She dug her fingers into his shoulders to anchor herself to him as her orgasm sent her into free fall.

Nico thrust deep, tensed and let out a savage groan as he exploded inside her, his big body shuddering with the force of his release. In the aftermath, as their breathing gradually slowed, a sweet lassitude swept over Sienna and once again she felt a sense of homecoming. This was where she belonged, whispered a little voice in her head, and her heart agreed.

What the hell had just happened? As Nico withdrew from Sienna he felt a sense of regret—not that he'd had sex with her but that it was over. He liked being buried deep inside her—although *liked* was an understatement. He'd just had the most amazing sexual experience of his life and astonishingly he was already hardening again. He enjoyed sex as much as any other red-blooded male. Women offered a pleasurable diversion and a release from tension—he was a self-confessed workaholic. But his affairs were always on his terms. Only Sienna made him mindless with desire. No other woman had ever made him lose control, and now that his hunger had been appeased—even if only temporarily—he felt a stirring of unease that she'd had such a devastating effect on him.

He was appalled by his lack of finesse. *Dio*, he hadn't even made it as far as the bed with her, he derided himself. He'd taken her up against the door with no consideration for her comfort or enjoyment. Although she *had* enjoyed it. Her moans of pleasure were still in his ears and his shoulders were stinging where she had dug her fingernails into his skin when she'd climaxed moments before his own incredible orgasm.

She lifted her face from the crook of his neck, her grey eyes still smoky with desire. But then she became aware of her surroundings, of what had just happened, and her expression turned wary. Nico's jaw tightened and he dismissed an odd sense of loss as he set her back down on her feet.

'I didn't take precautions,' he said roughly. Although he had reason to believe that he was infertile, it made sense not to take risks when he had sex. The fact that it hadn't even entered his mind to wear a condom when he'd thrust his way into Sienna's molten heat was further proof of his worrying lack of self-control with her.

'Precautions?' Her frown cleared and she gave him a wry glance. 'An unplanned pregnancy is not likely to be an issue for us, is it, Nico?'

The truth of her statement sent a lightning bolt of anger through him as it seemed to confirm his suspicion that she had known the child she'd been carrying when he'd married her had not been his.

'Pregnancy is not the only possible result of having unprotected sex,' he reminded her coolly. 'I am not usually so irresponsible.'

'Same here,' she mumbled, bending down to pick up her dress from the floor.

Nico had the feeling she wanted to avoid his gaze, as if she was embarrassed by what had happened.

'I don't normally behave like a tramp and leap into bed with a man at the first opportunity.' She was twisting her dress between her fingers, mangling the already crumpled silk. 'I don't know what came over me.'

He knew it was ridiculous to feel pleased by her admission that she did not make a habit of having casual sex. But she was in her late twenties and presumably she'd had other relationships in the past eight years. The fierce possessiveness that swept through him was inexplicable. After the divorce he had filed away their brief marriage as a mistake and moved on with his life. But he'd just proved that he was not completely over Sienna as he'd assumed.

'I must go.' She shook out her dress and grimaced at the sight of the badly creased silk. Her handbag was on the floor where she had dropped it. She frowned as she took out her phone. 'The battery has died. Would you mind calling a taxi for me? It will take ten minutes to walk to the village where I left my car, and I'll get soaked.'

The rumbles of thunder had quietened as the storm moved away but the rain was still hammering against the windows. It was completely dark now and Nico touched the remote-control panel on the wall to turn on the bedside lamps. Sienna blinked and he was intrigued by the soft colour that swept over her cheeks. She looked younger and vulnerable, stripped of her air of sophistication, and he felt a tug on his insides, possessiveness mixed with a fundamental urge to protect her.

'You used to like walking on the moors in the rain,' he murmured, brushing a few strands of hair back from her face. 'The first time we made love was on the moors in a thunderstorm. Do you remember?'

Her flush deepened but she ignored the question. 'I haven't got a change of clothes with me and I don't relish the thought of driving back to London in my dress that will be even wetter if I have to go outside in the rain.'

Seriously, did she expect him to send her on her way after he'd had his pleasure with her as if she were a hooker he'd picked up in a seedy bar? The idea that she had such a low opinion of him made him feel uncomfortable. He hadn't forced her to come to his room, he reminded himself. It had been her choice. And whether or not it was sensible, he wasn't ready to let her go yet.

He slid his hand beneath the heavy silk of her hair and curved his fingers around her nape. *'Idiota,'* he said gently. 'You'll stay here with me tonight.'

She bit her lip, drawing his attention to her mouth that was reddened and slightly swollen from where he had kissed her and where he was impatient to kiss her again. 'Nico, I can't.'

He heard determination in her voice but her eyes were as soft as woodsmoke, and a tremor ran through her when he tugged her dress out of her hands and drew circles around one dusky pink aureole with his fingertip. 'Tell me you don't want this and I will drive you to the village so that you can collect your car,' he told her, dipping his head so that his words grazed her lips.

She made a muffled sound somewhere between a sigh and groan, but she did not protest when he swept her up into his arms and carried her over to the bed. His heart thundered with triumph at her capitulation and anticipation that very soon he would slake his desire for her again. Maybe he was this hungry because he hadn't had sex for a couple of months after he'd ended an affair that had run its course. Celibacy was not a natural state for him, Nico acknowledged wryly.

He pulled back the bedspread and laid Sienna down on the pure silk sheets before he quickly stripped off his clothes and stretched out beside her. Emotions he refused to examine, much less define, swirled inside him as he spread her burgundy hair across the snowy white pillows.

When she was younger, Sienna had been so slender that she'd looked as breakable as spun glass. In the intervening years her figure had softened to a symphony of sexy curves that Nico was eager to explore. He could not bring himself to regret that he had made love to her. But once wasn't enough.

The night was long, and he planned to have her in as many varied ways as his imagination could conjure, taking them both to the absolute extremes of sexual satisfaction. And he fully expected that by the morning his desire for his little liar of an ex-wife would be sated once and for all.

CHAPTER FOUR

FROM THE TRAIN CARRIAGE, Sienna watched the picturesque Yorkshire countryside flash past the window.
Her phone pinged to announce she had a new text
message and her heart lurched when a number she
did not recognise flashed onto the screen.

Maybe it was from Nico? She'd heard nothing
from him for the past month and had almost given
up hope that he would get in touch. She had even
stopped checking her texts and emails quite so ob-
sessively. Although to be fair she hadn't left him her
number when she'd sneaked out of Sethbury Hall at
first light on the morning after she'd spent the night
with him. He had fallen asleep after he'd made love
to her for a fourth time, leaving her body quiver-
ing and her mind in turmoil. Her grand plan to have
sex with him to get him out of her system had back-
fired, and she'd feared that she was hopelessly addicted to him.

When faced with danger, most species, including

humans, went into fight-or-flight mode. Sienna had chosen to flee. She'd waited until Nico's breathing had slowed before she'd eased out from beneath his arm that he'd draped across her waist as if he wanted to anchor her to him. It was that kind of dangerous wishful thinking that had spurred her to scramble into her horribly creased dress and gather up her shoes and handbag. She couldn't find her knickers and had given up looking for them when Nico stirred.

Pausing in the doorway, she had looked back at him sprawled on the bed, one arm across his face, the sheet over his thighs and just covering his man-hood that unbelievably had still been semi-aroused. She'd remembered when they were married she had often lain awake at night and watched him sleeping, hardly able to believe that he was hers.

The truth was he never had been hers. She under-stood that now. But at eighteen she had been so in love with him that she'd ignored the rumours flying around the village that Nico had only married her because she had been pregnant and he'd been under pressure from his grandfather to claim the future heir to the Sethbury estate.

In the end there had not been a child. She had suf-fered a miscarriage in the fifth month of her preg-nancy and their tiny son had been stillborn. Luigi's grave was marked by a simple headstone in St Au-gustine's churchyard. Sienna swallowed the lump that had formed in her throat. She had been heartbroken, and even though many years had passed, the grief she'd felt for her baby, who had been so perfect that he had looked like a little doll, still felt like a knife in her heart.

She read the text message on her phone.

Have fitted a new brake cable on your car. Vehicle is ready for you to collect.

The message was from the garage where she had taken her car for a routine service. Swallowing her disappointment, she quickly checked for any new emails in her inbox but there was nothing from Nico. If he had wanted to contact her, he could have searched for her website on the Internet. When they had chatted over dinner at his brother's wedding reception, she had told him that she co-owned an organic skincare business called Fresh Faced.

The fact that she hadn't heard from him since he had taken her apart in his bed was proof, if she'd needed it, that she was a fool. There had always been a white-hot chemistry between them but she couldn't accuse Nico of taking advantage of her or making false promises. They'd had amazing sex but that was all it had been. It was time she stopped fantasising that there had been a special connection when they'd made love and put the night with Nico out of her mind, as he had clearly done.

It was a ten-minute walk from York train sta-

tion to the care home where Grandma Rose lived
semi-independently in a private suite of rooms. On
the way, Sienna collected the birthday cake she had
ordered from a bakery and stopped at a florist's to
buy a bunch of flowers. At Heath Lodge she gave
her name at Reception before taking the lift up to the
fourth floor. Juggling her overnight bag, the flowers
and the boxed cake, she turned the door handle and
entered her grandmother's rooms.

'Hi, Nanna, it's me.' She walked into the sitting
room and came to an abrupt halt when she saw Nico
standing by the window. Her first instinct was to bolt
and only her stubborn pride stopped her from running out of the door. From across the room she felt
the searing intensity of his gaze burn through her
cotton sundress. At least this time she was wearing
a bra, she thought.

She belatedly noticed his grandmother Iris was
sitting in an armchair next to Grandma Rose. 'Oh,
you're having a birthday party! Lucky I brought
a cake.' Sienna cringed at the sound of her overly
bright voice. She forced her feet to walk further into
the room but she tripped on the edge of the rug and
the cake box slipped out of her hand. With lightning
reactions, Nico sprang forwards and caught it before
it hit the floor.

'I hope you don't mind us being here for Rose's
birthday celebration,' he murmured.

'Of course not. The more the merrier.' She smiled

gaily at Iris and prayed that her thundering heart wasn't audible to Nico and their respective grand-mothers.

'I managed to persuade Nico to stop working for the afternoon so that he could bring me to visit Rose,' Iris explained.

So he hadn't engineered the visit because he'd hoped to see her, Sienna registered, annoyed with herself for feeling disappointed. Of course Nico hadn't thought about her constantly for the past weeks as she had thought about him. She wished he would move away from her. The spicy scent of his aftershave made her head spin. It didn't help that he looked utterly gorgeous in black jeans and a cream polo shirt, open at the neck to reveal a vee of tanned skin and a sprinkling of black chest hair.

'I'd better put your flowers in water,' she told Rose. Her eyes were drawn to the exquisite bouquet of roses, lilies and exotic orchids in a vase on the table. The stunning floral display made her bunch of yellow chrysanthemums seem very ordinary.

'Aren't they lovely? Nico bought them for me,' her grandmother said, following her gaze. 'It was very kind of you, Nico.' Rose gave him a fond smile. 'You already do so much for me. I wouldn't have been able to move into Heath Lodge without your help.'

Frowning, Sienna spun around from Saint Nico and headed into the little kitchen, saying, 'I'll make tea.'

'I'll help.' He followed her, and while she filled the kettle he leaned against the kitchen unit, his tall frame dominating the small space.

Waiting for the kettle to boil, Sienna muttered, 'What did my grandmother mean?'

He hesitated for a moment. 'I pay the fees so that Rose can live at Heath Lodge.'

'What?' She could not hide her shock. 'Why? Nanna sold her cottage before she moved here and I assumed she uses the proceeds to pay the care home's monthly fees.'

'A few years ago Rose took out a loan and put her cottage up as collateral. She gave the money to your father to try to prop up his pub business, but the pub failed, and Clive never repaid her.'

Sienna grimaced. 'That sounds like my father. The last I heard of him, he had moved to Ireland and was working in a friend's bar, probably drinking all the profits. I'm glad Mum finally found the courage to leave him.' She poured boiling water into the teapot and tried not to react when Nico passed her the milk and his fingers brushed against hers, sending a jolt of electricity up her arm. 'Why are you involved? Rose isn't your responsibility. If I had known about her money problems I'd have covered the care home's fees.'

'She didn't want to trouble you while you were establishing your business. When I heard about your grandmother's financial situation I was happy to help.' Nico's eyes narrowed. 'Why does my helping Rose bother you?'

'You shouldn't have to. It's not as if she is your relative.'

'My grandmother has been friends with your grandmother for many years and when you became my wife, our families had a closer connection. If you had accepted a divorce settlement from me, your financial situation would have been easier.' He frowned. 'Why did you return the cheque my solicitor sent you?'

'I didn't want anything from you. If I'd accepted the cheque it would have added weight to the rumours in the village that I had married you for your money.' Sienna loaded a tray with cups and saucers and set the sugar bowl down with a clatter. 'There were even whispers that I'd deliberately got pregnant so you would have to marry me.'

'Did you?'

She stared at him, wondering if she had heard him correctly. He stared back at her, his blue eyes coolly assessing and causing a little shiver to run down her spine. 'Of course I didn't. My pregnancy was an accident. A one-off miracle, as it turned out,' she said huskily, remembering her heartache after the miscarriage when she'd failed to conceive again. 'You didn't wear a condom the first time we made love up on the moors,' she reminded him. A decade later, the memory of their wild passion when he'd tumbled her down in the heather and they had frantically ripped each other's clothes off still heated her blood.

Nico gave her a warning look and she bit her lip, aware that Rose and Iris were within earshot. Lowering her voice, she said curtly, 'I can't believe we are having this discussion now. If you'd thought I had trapped you, why didn't you say so ten years ago? But the gossip in Much Matcham was partly right. The only reason you married me was because I was expecting your child, but when I failed to give you an heir there was no reason to continue with the marriage that you hadn't wanted. That's the truth, isn't it, Nico?'

Sienna sounded so convincing that Nico almost believed her. Almost. But he knew what a clever liar she was. He'd had no reason to think the baby she had been expecting wasn't his. She had told him she was a virgin before they'd made love for the first time, and he'd been surprised and delighted by her fiery passion that matched his own. He'd never suspected that she had slept with his brother just a week earlier.

'Why didn't you say that she was playing us both along?' he'd asked, when he'd confided his marriage problems to his brother and Danny had admitted that he and Sienna had got together before Nico had arrived in Much Matcham that summer ten years ago.

'I had gone to Monte Carlo the day before you

turned up at Sethbury Hall,' his brother had reminded him. 'By the time I came home you had announced your engagement to Sienna, and everyone knew she was expecting your baby. There didn't seem any point in mentioning that I'd had a fling with her. I figured that if she had wanted you to know she would have told you herself.'

Instead Sienna had fooled him into believing that he was the father of her unborn child, Nico thought darkly. He had been twenty-four and the idea of fatherhood had been terrifying. Another responsibility to add to his list. He was the oldest son and heir to his English and Italian family's fortunes and he'd grown up knowing that one day he would be in charge of Sethbury Hall and estate, as well as the hotel business De Conti Leisure. The weight of expectation on him was huge. When he had looked at the grainy scan image of his baby son he'd felt overwhelmed rather than excited.

His father's unexpected death a mere three months after Nico had learned that he was going to be a father himself had been a terrible shock. But more shocking still had been the discovery that Franco De Conti had fathered several illegitimate children while he had been married to Nico's mother.

Memories that Nico had suppressed for years forced their way into his mind. In the months after his father's death he had been under intense emotional strain when he'd flown to California on a business trip. But within hours of his plane landing, he'd received a phone call from the hospital in York where Sienna had been taken by ambulance after she'd started to bleed heavily. It had been Nico's grandmother who had broken the news that his baby son had been stillborn.

Numb with shock, he'd immediately flown back to England. Sienna had been utterly distraught, but Nico felt frozen inside, and even when he'd been taken by a nurse to see his lifeless baby there had been a sense of unreality. He had not held his child, but when he'd walked out of the room Nico had heard the ragged sound of his own breathing. He'd felt like he had run a marathon and his heart was about to burst out of his chest. Somehow he'd got himself together, knowing that he must support Sienna. But her grief had made him feel helpless, just as he'd felt helpless when he was a young boy and his mother had sobbed because of his father's infidelity.

They had named the baby Luigi, and held a funeral for him a week later. But once again it had felt unreal standing in the graveyard of St Augustine's church. Nico's throat had felt raw as if he'd swallowed broken glass when he held a weeping Sienna in his arms, but he hadn't cried. He couldn't. Tears and uncontrolled emotions terrified him. Nico's way of dealing with his emotions was to ignore them, but Sienna had accused him of being distant and uncaring. Then, when she'd failed to fall pregnant again and had become obsessed with ovulation charts and tips to improve fertility, he'd believed that she only wanted sex with him in order to conceive another child.

One thing he found puzzling was why Sienna had refused the generous divorce settlement he had instructed his lawyer to offer her. Although their marriage had been over he had still felt responsible for her. He'd supposed she had named him as the father of her child rather than Danny because he'd been in line to inherit the title of Viscount Mandeville. Perhaps Sienna had fancied herself as a viscountess. But in that case why had she walked away from their marriage with nothing?

Since the divorce Nico had pushed the question to the back of his mind. But a few moments ago Sienna had sounded hurt by the rumours that had abounded in Much Matcham at the time of their wedding that she had gone to extreme lengths to secure herself a rich husband.

Even more puzzling and infuriating was that for the past month Nico had been unable to forget the night they had spent together. The sex had blown him away. *Dio*, she was hot. He had woken the next morning to the pleasurable ache of over-used muscles, and he had been hard again, his body clenching with anticipation of a leisurely morning ride with his very sexy ex.

Maybe it had been so good because their bodies

had recognised each other's, and had known how to give and receive the most intense satisfaction. He had realised that one night with Sienna was not going to be enough. An affair was the obvious answer but she would have to understand that there were rules and boundaries. Commitment was not something he sought or could offer.

He had rolled over in the four-poster bed, impatient to pull her beneath him. But there had been an empty space on the mattress and a faint indentation on the pillow where her head had lain. The en-suite bathroom had been empty, and when he had walked back into the bedroom he'd discovered that her clothes had gone, except for a pair of lace knickers that he found on the floor when he picked up his shirt. Sienna, it seemed, had her own rules, and Nico had assured himself that he was relieved to avoid a tedious conversation about expectations that, in his experience, most women harboured.

Jerking his mind from his tangled thoughts, he followed her into the sitting room. She had placed the tea tray on a low table and was sitting on the sofa facing the two elderly ladies who occupied the armchairs. Nico lowered his tall frame onto the only vacant seat next to Sienna on the small sofa and felt her tense when his thigh inadvertently brushed against hers. The knowledge that he unsettled her was a salve to his wounded pride when he had woken after the most incredible night of his life and discovered that she had walked away from him *again*.

Sienna busied herself by pouring the tea. 'Did you enjoy Danny's wedding?' Iris asked her. 'I looked for you in the marquee after dinner, but I couldn't see you.'

'I had to leave the reception early to drive back to London.' A pink stain swept along Sienna's cheekbones and Nico was amused when she avoided his gaze.

'Actually I have something of yours that you left behind.' He slipped his hand into the pocket of his jacket, which was hanging over the arm of the sofa, and handed her a little cardboard box tied with ribbon. When she stared at it warily, he murmured, 'It's wedding cake. Every guest was given a slice. What were you expecting, *cara*?'

Her blush deepened and he knew she had feared that he had been about to return her underwear that she had left in his bedroom. It would certainly have added fuel to their grandmothers' curiosity. The memory of how he had ripped Sienna's panties off and made love to her, hard and fast, up against the bedroom door sent desire corkscrewing through him.

It was no use fighting his desire for Sienna. He must have her again, Nico decided. She had got under his skin and he wanted to ruffle her composure. She was so cool sitting there with a faint smile playing on her lips as if she was aware that he was painfully hard beneath his jeans. So she found it amusing that she tied him in knots, did she? But he could play games too. He shifted in his seat to try to alleviate the throb of his erection and stretched his arm along the back of the sofa, bringing his body into closer contact with hers.

The pulse beating frantically at the base of her throat betrayed her awareness of him and he fought an urge to press his lips to the fragile line of her collarbone. He was desperate to be alone with her, but he reminded himself that Sienna had come to Yorkshire to visit her grandmother and he would have to be patient.

Iris spoke again. 'I remember you said at the wedding that you needed to prepare for an important business meeting, Sienna. Was the meeting successful?'

Suppressing a sigh of relief, Sienna seized on the safe topic of work, hoping it would distract her from Nico's brooding presence beside her. She wished he would move his arm from the back of the sofa. The scent of his aftershave teased her senses. He was too big, too close, too overwhelming. He made her feel like a silly teenager again with a massive crush on him.

'Yes, I persuaded the managing director of a chain of beauty salons to stock my range of organic skincare products,' she told Nico's grandmother. She was proud of her business that she'd built into a thriving company from the early days when she'd come up with the idea of Fresh Faced and developed a few products, which she'd sold online.

'I was telling Iris how you use a special ingredient that comes from an African fruit in your skin creams,' Grandma Rose said.

'Marula oil is the base of most of the products we make at Fresh Faced. The Marula trees grow mainly in southern Africa and the yellow fruits they produce are about the size of a peach,' Sienna explained. 'The fruits have a large nut inside, and it is from the nut that the Marula oil is extracted.'

'I assume you import the oil into the UK, and then do you have a laboratory or workshop where your products are manufactured?' Nico asked.

'The workshop is in London—at Camden Lock by the Regent's Canal. I employ a small team of three people, and all the products are handmade using fresh, organic ingredients. The Marula oil we use is sourced from Tutjo. It's a small African state bordering Namibia and South Africa,' Sienna said when Iris looked puzzled.

'At Fresh Faced we work with a women's cooperative in Tutjo and abide by the Fairtrade standards. The women harvest the Marula fruit and using basic tools they remove the nut, crack it open and collect the kernels, which are then cold-pressed to produce Marula oil. There is no mass production, it's all done by the village women, and Fresh Faced donates twenty-five per cent of the company's profits to the cooperatives to support health and education for women and children in Tutjo.'

Iris shook her head. 'What a fascinating job you have, Sienna. I must admit that I have never heard of Marula fruit, or, for that matter, Tutjo. Have you visited there?'

'Several times, and I'm planning to go again later this year.'

Nico frowned. 'The King of Tutjo has ruled for decades, but I've heard reports of increased unrest in the country and a while ago there was a threat of a military coup.'

'I believe things have settled down now. My partner, Brent, lives in South Africa and he follows the political situation in Tutjo closely. It's a poor country but the cooperatives offer women a chance to earn an income, which many of them use to pay for their children to be educated. I'm proud that Fresh Faced helps women to be independent. It's something I feel very strongly about.'

The conversation moved on to other subjects but Sienna continued to be fiercely aware of Nico. A few times she glanced at him and caught him looking at her intently as if he was trying to fathom her out. She was almost relieved when she noticed Rose's eyelids droop. Her grandmother was ninety-one and tired easily, although her mind was as sharp as ever.

'Nanna, I'm going to go and check into my hotel. I'll come back tomorrow and we'll go out somewhere for lunch.'

'Come and have lunch at Sethbury Hall,' Iris invited. 'I'll send Hobbs in the Bentley to collect both of you.'

'Oh, that's very kind of you, but we couldn't impose.' Sienna sent Nico a silent appeal for help. She was sure he did not want to extend the awkward afternoon over to the following day any more than she did.

'That's an excellent idea.' He ignored her frown and smiled at her grandmother. 'I expect you would like to see Much Matcham again, Rose. Shall we say lunch at one o'clock?'

The invitation did not mean that Nico wanted to see *her* again, Sienna told herself firmly after she had kissed her grandmother goodbye. Nico followed her into the lift, pushing his grandmother in her wheelchair. When they exited the care home a silver Bentley pulled up alongside them. 'Nico arranged for Hobbs to drive me home because he has some business in York,' Iris explained.

The chauffeur helped the elderly lady into the car and after it had driven away Sienna hooked the strap of her holdall over her shoulder. 'I guess I'll see you tomorrow,' she muttered, wondering what kind of business Nico planned to do. Perhaps he had a mistress in York and would spend the night with her. Jealousy jabbed like a sharp knife in her stomach.

Nico had donned a pair of designer sunglasses and he looked very Italian and sexier than ever. Years ago she had been infatuated with him but at eighteen she'd had no experience of the world, Sienna reminded herself. Now she understood that he belonged to an exclusive breed of powerful men who lived life by their own rules. Rich, handsome and charismatic, Nico could have any woman he wanted, but he refused to be owned and any woman who tried would end up with a broken heart as she had done.

'My car is parked over there.' He nodded to a silver sports car. 'I'll give you a lift to your hotel. Where are you staying?'

'The Arlington. It's only a five-minute walk from here. I always stay there when I visit Rose.'

He fell into step beside her as she walked along the street and lifted her bag from her shoulder before she could argue. 'I didn't want to say too much in front of your grandmother but you should think seriously about visiting Tutjo. The Foreign Office's advice is to only travel to that region of Africa if it is absolutely essential.'

'The advice was recently updated and currently the travel risk to Tutjo is low.'

'Even so, it would be better if you postponed your trip.'

She stopped walking and swung round to face

him. 'I'm not your responsibility, Nico. If we hadn't met at Danny's wedding you wouldn't know anything about my travel plans.'

His eyes glittered. 'But we did meet and we ended up in bed. I haven't been able to forget that amazing night, *cara*, and I suspect the same is true for you.'

'You are so arrogant…' she began, her voice faltering when he lifted his hand and brushed his thumb pad lightly over her cheek.

'The dark circles beneath your eyes suggest that you haven't been sleeping well recently.'

'And naturally you assume that I've stayed awake every night thinking about you,' she said tartly. 'Maybe my restless nights were for another reason.'

His gaze cooled to the chilly blue of an Arctic sky. 'Were you thinking of your lover in South Africa? This Brent guy who you said is your partner,' he growled when she looked puzzled.

'Brent is my brother-in-law. He's Allie's husband and my business partner.' Sienna ran her fingers through her hair, pushing the long layered style back from her face. She wondered why Nico suddenly looked tense. 'After the divorce I went to stay with my sister and her husband at their home in South Africa. Brent is an environmental scientist and was already working with women's cooperatives in Tutjo. Allie had become interested in natural skincare lotions after she developed very bad eczema and she is allergic to most of the synthetic chemicals found in beauty products.

'I'd graduated with a degree in business and marketing before I left England, and I went on to qualify in organic skincare formulation. My sister has taken a step back from the business since she has become a mother.'

Sienna could not hide the tremor in her voice. She adored her two little nephews, but when she'd held them soon after they were born, her arms had ached to cradle her own child. 'Two years ago I moved back to the UK to establish a base for Fresh Faced in Europe.'

They had reached her hotel and she held out her hand to take her bag from Nico, but he kept hold of it and opened the door so that she could precede him into the lobby. 'What's it like here?' he said, casting a curious look around the smart, boutique hotel.

'It's not bad. It was originally a private Victorian house with rooms in the attic where the scullery maids slept. The hotel offers small, single rooms at a cheap rate—small being the key word,' she said ruefully. 'But I only need a bed to sleep in when I come to York to visit Grandma Rose.'

An unbidden memory popped into her mind of Nico's huge four-poster bed at Sethbury Hall. They had barely slept at all the night she had spent with him. His gaze sharpened on her flushed face and he seemed to have the ability to read her thoughts. 'Why did you leave without waking me?' he asked abruptly.

She shrugged. 'I didn't want a post-mortem any more than I imagine you did. What happened was crazy but it was just sexual chemistry.' That was what she had repeatedly told herself for the past month. 'It seemed like a good idea to forget it ever happened.'

'But you haven't succeeded in forgetting the night we spent together.'

'Yes, I have,' she snapped, riled by his superior tone. 'Just as you obviously haven't given me another thought.' His failure to phone her even just once to check that she had got back to London safely had hurt, dammit.

'If that was the case I wouldn't have cut short a business trip to Brussels so that I could bring Iris to have tea with your grandmother, when I heard that you would be visiting Rose this weekend,' he said drily.

Did he mean it? She did not know how to respond, and luckily the receptionist at the desk became free after she had finished dealing with another guest. Sienna completed the check-in procedure and when she looked round she discovered that Nico had gone. He had left her holdall on the floor by her feet. There was just lunch tomorrow to get through and then she would never have to see him again, she consoled herself as she walked over to the lift. The budget-rate rooms were on the fifth floor and she did not intend to take the stairs.

'Miss Fisher.' Sienna turned her head and saw the receptionist hurrying towards her. 'I'm so sorry, I allocated you the wrong room. You will be staying in the Executive Suite on the first floor.'

'I think there must be a mistake,' Sienna began.

The receptionist looked flustered. 'Um…it's a free upgrade to thank you for being a loyal guest.'

Bemused, Sienna allowed the porter who had appeared at her side to carry her holdall and when the lift stopped at the first floor she followed him along the corridor. He opened a door and ushered her into the suite. 'If you require anything, please dial two on the phone for room service.'

The upgraded room was bound to be a mistake, she thought as she looked around the charming open-plan suite. Something as nice as this did not happen to her. For years she'd survived on a shoestring until her skincare business had taken off, and although she now earned a reasonable salary, she couldn't justify paying for a luxurious suite.

Next to the bed there was an enormous, free-standing bath with views out of the window over the river. The idea of a long soak to ease the tension in her neck and shoulders was inviting. She turned on the taps and added a liberal splash of rose-scented bubble bath from the Fresh Faced range of travel-size toiletries that she had brought with her. It seemed rather decadent to take a bath in the afternoon, she thought guiltily as she undressed and piled her hair on top of her head, securing it with a couple of pins. Usually she would be hard at work—even at weekends.

Lying back in the foamy water, she wondered if she could persuade the hotel manager to stock some of her company's products. Business was never far from Sienna's mind, and being financially independent was vital to her. When she was growing up her father had been a violent bully, but her mother had been trapped in the marriage because she did not have any qualifications or career prospects. Sienna had vowed never to allow any man to have power over her, but her determination to go to university had been another source of tension between her and Nico, she remembered.

She had started studying for a business degree soon after they had met. When she'd discovered that she was pregnant and Nico asked her to marry him, she had hoped to combine her studies with motherhood. But fate had delivered a cruel blow and after the miscarriage she had focused on gaining her degree to take her mind off the monthly disappointment when she failed to fall pregnant again.

With a sigh, Sienna sank deeper into the scented bubbles and let her mind drift back to the past. Nico had spent a lot of time in Italy after his father had died and he had taken over as CEO of De Conti Leisure. He'd asked her to go to Verona with him but she had wanted to remain in England to finish her degree. She had also wanted to stay close to her mother. Lynn Fisher had led a miserable life with her drunkard husband and had relied on Sienna after her older sister Allie had moved to South Africa.

Sienna had resented Nico's frequent trips to Italy and blamed his absences for her failure to conceive another baby. The truth was that they had married too young, she thought ruefully. Neither of them had been prepared to make compromises that might have given their relationship a chance.

A knock on the door of the suite pulled her mind back to the present and she jolted upright so that water sloshed over the sides of the bath when a voice called out, 'Room service.' She was startled when the door opened and hastily sank beneath the bubbles, aware that the bath was visible from the doorway.

'Go away. I didn't order anything.'

Her heart missed a beat when Nico strolled in, carrying a tray with a bottle of champagne and two glasses. The gleam of amusement in his eyes turned to something hotter and hungrier as he stared at her naked shoulders above the foam.

CHAPTER FIVE

IN AN INSTANT Sienna went from relaxed to fiercely aware of Nico and of her femininity. 'Did you arrange for my room to be upgraded?' she asked stiffly.

His mouth crooked in a sexy smile that stole her breath. 'I couldn't allow you stay in the attic where the scullery maids used to sleep.'

'It's no concern of yours where I sleep.' She could not take her eyes off him when he strolled across the room and put the tray of champagne down on a bedside table. Ten years ago she had been the modern equivalent of a scullery maid— a lowly cleaner at Sethbury Hall when Nico, the handsome heir to his family's ancestral home and a future viscount, had swept her off her feet. She had been desperately in love with him but he had not returned her love.

She opened her mouth to tell him to leave but the words stuck in her throat. There was a soft 'pop' of a cork as he opened the champagne. 'What shall we drink to?' he said when he had filled the two flutes and handed one of them to her. 'Old friendships, or new beginnings?'

'We were never friends, not really. On our wedding day we were virtually strangers.' Sienna took a sip of her champagne before she placed the glass on the windowsill. 'And this is not a new beginning.'

Nico's eyes burned into hers. 'What is it, then?'

It was madness, Sienna told herself. But her internal voice of caution was drowned out by the thunderous beat of her heart as she rested her hands on the edges of the roll-top bath and stood up. Water streamed down her body and the silken glide of it felt sensuous on her skin as each one of her nerve endings quivered with a need that was primitive and urgent. A woman calling to her man.

She removed the pins from her hair and tossed her head so that her hair swirled around her shoulders. 'It's just sex, isn't it, Nico.' It was a statement rather than a question. She was no longer a teenager with a head full of dreams. She understood that the emotion blazing in his blue eyes was lust, not love, and with that knowledge came power and freedom to do whatever she wanted to do.

What she wanted was Nico.

He had gone very still when she'd risen, naked and proud, from the bathwater. A nerve flickered in his cheek and he swallowed his champagne in a couple of gulps before placing the glass back on the tray.

'Right now, I don't give a damn what it is,' he

growled. 'All I can think about is being inside you.'
He ignored the towel she had draped over the towel
stand and scooped her wet body into his arms, lowering his head to capture her mouth in a fierce kiss
that was both a punishment and a promise.

It was even better than before, when they had
spent the night together at Sethbury Hall after his
brother's wedding. Maybe it was because she had
given up trying to fight her desire for Nico and accepted that she was a lost cause, Sienna thought.

He kissed her again as he laid her on the bed, and
when he straddled her, his knees on either side of her
body, she stopped thinking altogether. She wanted
to make love with him, although she was aware that
love—that dangerously beguiling emotion—was not
involved.

'I've made your shirt wet,' she murmured.

'You had better take it off, then.' His voice was
very deep, and when he sat back on his haunches and
stared down at her, the hard glitter in his eyes sent
a shiver of excitement through her. Impatient to get
her hands on his body, she gripped the hem of his
polo shirt and pulled it up. He helped her tug it over
his head and groaned when she skimmed her fingertips over his chest, traced the ridges of his impressive
abdominal muscles and continued down to unbuckle
the belt on his jeans. She did not hesitate or pretend
to be coy. She wanted him inside her, *now*.

But Nico would not be rushed and took his time

to explore every dip and curve on her body with his mouth. He kissed her throat and nuzzled the sensitive place behind her ear, returning between each caress to claim her lips with fierce passion and an underlying tenderness that tugged on her foolish heart. His foreplay was unhurried and exquisitely sensual. He played her body like a master musician and wrung husky moans of pleasure from her when at last, *at last* he kissed her breasts and sucked one nipple and then the other until both tips were hard and rosy red.

He stood up and stripped off the rest of his clothes before he stretched out beside her on the bed. Propping himself up on one elbow, he traced a lazy path with his finger down her body, paused to explore the indent of her navel before moving lower to the neat triangle of curls at the junction of her thighs. 'You are so beautiful.' His voice was soft, but when he slipped his hand between her legs and discovered the slick heat of her arousal, he smiled and murmured, 'You *are* eager, *cara*.'

His satisfied tone sent a little chill through Sienna. Nico was used to women falling at his feet—or rather into his bed—and although his eyes blazed with desire, something about his cool smile warned her to guard herself against his charisma.

She slid her hand down to clasp his powerful erection. 'So are you.' His breath hissed between his teeth when she tightened her fingers around his shaft. Taking advantage of his preoccupation, she moved suddenly and reversed their positions so that he was flat on his back and she was on top of him. She saw a flicker of surprise in his eyes and sensed that he was uncomfortable with the idea of relinquishing control.

'Kiss me,' he ordered, regarding her from between his half-closed eyelids. His head was thrown back against the pillows and he reminded her of an indolent sultan choosing a favourite concubine to pleasure him.

Once she would have covered him in kisses and been desperate to please him. She had been needy and immature, but thank goodness she had grown up, Sienna thought. At eighteen she had been too young and unsure of herself to get married. She had put Nico on a pedestal but he had his faults just as everyone did, and like most powerful men he was determined to take charge of every situation.

'Oh, I'll kiss you,' she murmured. But she evaded his hand when he tried to catch hold of a lock of her hair to pull her mouth down to his. She wriggled down his body, making him groan when she rubbed the tips of her breasts over his chest. He swore as she moved lower still and he realised what she intended to do.

'Not this time, *cara*. I'm too close to the edge,' he said harshly. She ignored him and ran her tongue along the length of his erection before she took the swollen tip into her mouth. He inhaled sharply.

'Witch.' He tried to roll her beneath him but she laughed and pushed him back against the pillows.

'You asked me to kiss you but you didn't specify where,' she teased him. 'You need to learn to let go of your iron self-control, Nico.'

'Are you going to teach me how?' he asked drily, but he could not disguise the thickness in his voice or the fierce glitter in his eyes.

'Why don't we find out?' she murmured before she put her mouth on him.

Sienna felt a shudder run through his big, taut body, and realised that she was shaking too. It seemed ridiculous that at the age of twenty-nine she had never done this before. During their marriage Nico had always taken the lead and ensured that sex was wonderfully fulfilling for her. He had built her up and taken her apart until she'd sobbed his name in the shattering ecstasy of every orgasm he gave her. Only when she'd been utterly wrung out had he taken his own pleasure, but his self-control had never cracked.

Once she had been a slave to her need for him, she thought ruefully. But now the harsh sound he made when she flicked her tongue across the tip of his manhood filled her with a heady sense of self-confidence. She would play the dominant role and bring Nico to his knees.

Shaking her hair back over her shoulders, she caressed his steel-hard length with her hands and mouth, ignoring his savage commands to stop what she was doing before it was too late.

Sienna hadn't expected that pleasuring him would be such a turn-on, and she concentrated on her task, encouraged by the laboured sound of his breathing. He stretched his arms out on either side of him and curled his fingers into the sheet as if to anchor himself to the bed. It gave her a thrill to know that this enigmatic man was at her mercy.

'Tesoro.' His voice was low and strained. He sank his fingers into her hair but did not attempt to pull her away from him. She continued to use her mouth on him and felt him start to shake. The explosion as he came was spectacular. He gave a shout that sounded as though it had been torn from his throat. Every muscle on his body tensed and he let out a groan that resonated deep inside Sienna's chest.

She lifted her head and silently told herself not to be stupid when she felt heat spread across her cheeks as she met Nico's gaze. She wished she knew what he was thinking but his handsome face gave nothing away.

'Why do I have the idea that you were proving a point?' he murmured.

Feeling oddly vulnerable, she inched across to the edge of the bed, but before she could stand up he snaked an arm around her waist. 'You're not thinking of running out on me again, are you, *piccola*?'

His voice was like rough velvet and she steeled

herself against the lure of his husky endearment. In the early days of their marriage Nico had often called her 'little one'. She had been so happy then; married to the man she adored and expecting his baby. But she had been heartbroken when she'd miscarried their son and, engulfed in grief, she had sensed a distance between her and Nico, which had seemed to prove that the rumours in Much Matcham had been right and he had only married her because she had been pregnant.

Sienna closed the door on painful memories of the past. 'I want some champagne.' She had left her drink on the windowsill. Nico picked up his glass from the bedside table and handed it to her. She took a few sips before she returned the glass to him and gasped when he poured the remainder of the champagne over her breasts.

The cold liquid had a predictable effect on her nipples and she did not need to glance down to know that they were as hard as pebbles. She felt a sharp tug of anticipation shoot down to her pelvis when he closed his mouth around one taut peak and sucked hard. Before she could blink, she found herself flat on her back. Nico pinned her wrists above her head with one of his hands and with his other he pushed her legs apart and stroked his fingers over her opening.

'You didn't think I would allow you to escape retribution, did you, *cara*?' he drawled. The gleam of amusement in his eyes darkened to desire as he settled himself between her thighs, bent his head and licked his way into her.

Nico had planned to take Sienna to dinner, but it was late in the evening when he reluctantly lifted himself off her after they had made love for a third, or maybe fourth time—he'd lost count. He called room service and ordered a meal to be sent up to the suite, and then he refilled the bath and joined her in the foamy water while they finished off the bottle of champagne.

'Why didn't you call me after Danny's wedding?' she asked him later, while they ate parmesan risotto with roasted shrimps.

Nico studied her across the table. She had pulled on a white towelling robe when she'd stepped out of the bath and he missed the sight of her naked body as much as he missed the feel of her soft limbs spread beneath him. She was so beautiful. When she ran a hand carelessly through her burgundy silk hair, he felt hunger gnaw in the pit of his stomach that food could not assuage.

Dio, when she'd pleasured him with her mouth he'd thought he had died and gone to heaven. He couldn't remember the last time he had lost control like that. Maybe never. He shoved away the idea that sex with his ex-wife had been more intense than it had with any of the women he'd slept with since their divorce. His relationships were always brief, sex-without-strings affairs, and he made it clear from the outset that commitment was not on the cards.

There had not been accusation in Sienna's voice, merely a mild curiosity. She was different from the girl he had married a decade ago, but how different?

He shrugged. 'I didn't want you to fall in love with me, or hope that I might fall in love with you.'

She stared at him and then said drily, 'It's lucky you arranged for my room to be upgraded to the biggest suite in the hotel. Your swollen head wouldn't fit into anywhere smaller.'

So—no pout, or tantrum, or eyes filling with tears. Nico's lips twitched at her comment and he slowly relaxed. He hated tears especially. His earliest boyhood memories were of his mother crying. 'Your father doesn't love me,' she had told him when he'd climbed onto her bed and patted her heaving shoulders, trying to comfort her. 'How can Franco treat me like this? My life is not worth living now he has broken my heart,' Jacqueline had sobbed. 'And all for a cheap little tart half his age.'

Worse than the crying had been the drug overdoses, Nico thought grimly. He had been older by then. Only eleven or twelve, but old enough to understand that his mother had attempted to take her own life by swallowing a handful of sleeping pills. The first incident had happened after his parents had officially separated and his father moved to Paris

to live with his French mistress. The next time his
mother had tried to kill herself had been the day after
Franco De Conti had married an American actress.

Nico remembered his grandparents' distress when
their only daughter had been in intensive care. He
had dreaded that his mother might die, but he'd had
to be strong for Danny, and he'd hidden his emotions—a trait that he had carried into adulthood. He
was the oldest, and it had been his responsibility to
protect his younger brother from the drama and acrimony of their parents' hellish marriage.

'Why do you make Mama unhappy?' Nico had
once asked his father.

Franco had given an eloquent shrug of his shoulders. Women did not understand that it was unnat-
ural for a man to remain faithful to one woman, he
had advised his teenage son. Nico would learn that
women had impossible expectations.

His father had been right. By the time Nico had
developed from a boy to a young man, he'd discovered that women were fascinated with him and he
had not had to try very hard to persuade them to fall
into his bed. Unfortunately many of them had also
fallen in love with him and expected him to return
their feelings. When he had met Sienna ten years ago,
their sexual chemistry had blazed out of control before he'd had a chance to establish the rules of their
relationship. Her pregnancy had catapulted him into
a marriage he had not been ready for.

Sienna had said that they were strangers on their wedding day and in many ways it was true, he acknowledged. They had both kept secrets, but Nico had been aware that she was in love with him and he had been afraid that he would hurt her as his father had so often hurt his mother.

'There's no need to get worked up, Nico.' Sienna's voice pulled him back to the present. 'You are the last man on the planet I'd fall in love with.'

The amusement in her tone rankled. Naturally he was relieved by her assurance, but 'worked up'? Had she been making a subtle reference to the way he'd lost control so spectacularly when she had given him a blow job?

Nico's jaw tightened. Inexplicably he was tempted to ask her why she was so certain she wouldn't fall for him. He hadn't been *that* bad a husband. When Sienna had been his wife, he had bought her beautiful clothes and jewellery and she had lived in luxurious surroundings at Sethbury Hall.

'Would you like coffee?' he asked when they had both finished eating. She nodded and he carried the tray containing a cafetière over to the low table in front of the sofa. Sienna joined him, curling up on the sofa and tucking her feet beneath her. Nico poured the coffee and handed her a cup.

'I shouldn't have caffeine this late. I'll be awake all night,' she said ruefully.

'That's the idea, *cara*,' he drawled. 'Why do you think the Italians invented coffee?'

She laughed, and the husky sound fanned the flames of Nico's desire once more. 'You were on my mind a lot over the past month,' he admitted. If he was honest he had expected her to contact him. She knew the phone number for Sethbury Hall, and he had told his housekeeper to give Sienna Fisher his mobile number if she called. But she hadn't. 'Did you think about me?'

She shrugged. 'I've been very busy lately.'

Her cool tone irked him, but the soft colour that touched her cheekbones was an indication that her answer hadn't been completely honest. He stretched out his hand and idly wound a lock of her hair around his finger. 'You were busy at work?'

'Mmm.'

Why was she avoiding his gaze? Did she have a lover in London who kept her busy? Nico stiffened as the unwelcome thought slid into his mind. It was obvious from the way she became a wildcat when they made love that she was sexually experienced. *Dio*, maybe she had gifted the same pleasure she'd given him with her mouth and wicked tongue to a boyfriend. Acid burned a corrosive path down to the pit of his stomach. Indigestion, he told himself. It was certainly not jealousy.

'After we divorced I thought you might have re-married and had a family.' He kept his tone casual.

She gave another laugh but this time it sounded brittle and faintly bitter. 'I'm sure you've heard the saying once bitten, twice shy. I've seen enough bad marriages, including my parents' travesty of a marriage, to put me off wanting to go down that road again. As for having a family of my own, I've had to come to terms with my inability to have a child.'

The slight unsteadiness of her voice suggested to Nico that she wasn't being entirely truthful. He frowned. 'You sound as though you blame yourself because we couldn't have a baby. But you shouldn't,' he said shortly.

'We split up before we were due to start tests to investigate why I couldn't conceive, but I think it could be a genetic problem. Grandma Rose told me that after she had my dad, she hoped to have more children, but she couldn't fall pregnant again.'

Surely Sienna must have realised that the problems they had experienced were nothing to do with her, Nico brooded. It did not take a science degree to work out that she had fallen pregnant by his brother but she hadn't conceived a child with him even though they had tried for a year. He forced himself to concentrate when she spoke again.

'I guess you could say that my business is my baby substitute,' she said wryly. 'Fresh Faced was my idea, and it's been a hard slog to break into the skincare market, which is already crowded. But I believe absolutely in the ethos of the company and what we are trying to achieve. Working with the women's cooperatives in Tutjo to develop wonderful products that are kind to humans and the environment has taken over my life for the past few years. The only downside is that I haven't had much time for relationships.'

'But you have had other lovers?' Of course she had, Nico told himself. Sienna was a beautiful and highly sensual woman. He shouldn't give a damn that she must have shared her exquisite body with other men. He *didn't* give a damn. 'Out of interest, how many?' he heard himself ask.

She gave him a cool smile but he felt tension in the fine bones of her shoulders when he moved his hand up to cup her nape. 'Not as many as you, I'm sure,' she said lightly. 'Why do you care, Nico?'

'I don't,' he lied. 'I merely wanted to make sure that I'm not stepping on another man's toes.' At her frown, he elaborated. 'You might have a boyfriend in London.'

'I don't.' Her gaze turned stormy. 'If I did I wouldn't have slept with you. But now that you have mentioned the subject, are you currently having sex with anyone?'

'Not currently,' he murmured, his hands untying the belt of her robe. He watched her grey eyes darken, the pupils dilating when he bared her breasts and rubbed his thumb pads over her nipples, making them swell and harden. 'Ask me again in twenty seconds from now and I can guarantee my answer will be different,' he whispered against her mouth. She made a muffled sound that might have been a protest, but her lips parted beneath his and Nico's heart slammed into his ribs as the magic started all over again.

A long time later, after Sienna had fallen asleep and Nico lay beside her while his heart rate gradually returned to normal, he acknowledged that having sex with her again had not satisfied his hunger for her. She was like a narcotic in his blood and he needed her.

The thought made him frown. Of course he wasn't addicted to Sienna. He did not need any woman, and certainly not his traitorous ex-wife. But there was no reason why he shouldn't enjoy her mind-blowing sensuality for a few more nights, until what was new and exciting became familiar and mundane, as his affairs invariably did. And then he would have no problem walking away from Sienna, he assured himself.

Lunch at Sethbury Hall the next day turned out not to be the ordeal that Sienna had dreaded. By tacit consent she and Nico made no reference to the fact that they had spent the previous night together. She certainly didn't want Rose or Iris to think that a reunion between them was likely. Which of course it wasn't, she reminded herself. At the most, she and Nico would have an affair that they both knew from the start would end. He was gorgeous, but she would not be foolish enough to fall in love with him again.

Although she'd had to remind herself to guard her heart against him when he had woken her in the morning with a kiss that had quickly become a ravishment of her senses. He had made love to her with such passion, coupled with an aching tenderness that could have tricked her into believing that he had missed her as much as she had missed him for the last eight years.

They did not get up until late morning, and he gave her another lingering kiss before he finally departed from the hotel suite. Sienna raced into the shower before donning a green silk wrap dress that complemented the dark red of her hair.

'You look as bright as a button,' her grandmother commented when they were travelling in the chauffeur-driven Bentley that had come to collect them from York. 'Did you sleep well?'

Luckily they arrived at Sethbury Hall and Sienna mumbled a reply, trying to hide the blush that she could feel spreading across her face when Nico came down the front steps to meet them. He was wearing close-fitting black trousers and a black shirt with the sleeves rolled up to his elbows. The gold watch glinting on his wrist nestled among the black hairs that covered his tanned forearms. Sienna immediately visualised the whorls of black hair that grew thickly on his chest.

'Rose, welcome to Sethbury Hall,' he greeted her grandmother, before he turned his attention to her. 'It's good to see you again, Sienna.' He captured her hand and lifted it up to his mouth, brushing his lips over her knuckles and sending a sizzle of electricity down to her toes. 'You look lovely. I trust you slept well.'

'Everyone is obsessed with how I slept,' she said lightly. Inside, she was furious with herself for blushing again.

'I admit I'm obsessed with you,' Nico murmured in a soft voice. Sienna hoped her grandmother did not notice her scarlet cheeks when she took Rose's arm and helped her climb the steps up to the house.

During lunch she focused her attention on the two elderly ladies. She had become fond of Iris when she had lived at Sethbury Hall as Nico's wife and she adored her grandmother, whose husband and son had both been heavy drinkers. Despite the many difficulties in her life, Grandma Rose was one of the most resilient women Sienna had ever met.

'What time is your train?' Nico asked later when he found her outside on the terrace. Despite her best efforts to appear composed during lunch, Sienna had been agonisingly aware of him sitting next to her, and she had barely eaten anything, which had prompted her grandmother to ask if she was feeling unwell. In fact she had felt nauseous for the last couple of days, but she had put it down to the current heatwave in what was being called one of England's hottest summers.

'I don't have a return ticket,' she told him. 'I'd planned to catch a flight from Leeds airport to France later today and spend tomorrow researching possible sites for a new workshop for Fresh Faced in Paris, before a business meeting on Monday morning. But the meeting has been cancelled so I'll postpone my research and aim to catch the four o'clock train back to London.'

She glanced at him and flushed when her gaze crashed into his. Memories of their wild passion the previous night flooded her mind, and the gleam in his eyes warned her that he could read her thoughts. She cleared her throat. 'It was nice to meet you this weekend.'

His brows lifted. 'Nice? I am mortified, *cara*.'

Oh, hell. The way his mouth crooked at the corners when he smiled made her melt. 'Stop fishing for compliments,' she told him, drowning in the deep blue pools of his eyes. He was utterly irresistible, she thought with a flash of despair.

'Come to Italy with me.'

She stared at him, her heart thudding painfully hard. 'Why?'

'I'm hosting a cocktail party at the villa at Lake Garda this evening for my senior executive team. The party will only be for a few hours,' he murmured, moving closer and winding a lock of her hair around his finger. 'The truth, *cara*, is that I will spend every minute of those hours trying to curb my impatience to take you to bed.'

His face was so close to hers that she felt his warm breath brush across her lips. The scent of his aftershave tantalised Sienna's senses and the undisguised hunger in his eyes sent a shudder of longing through her. She lifted her hand to his chest, wishing she could rip off his shirt and touch his satiny skin beneath it. She would be crazy to agree to go to Italy with him.

'I don't have anything with me to wear to a party,' she said distractedly, willing him to lower his mouth a few more centimetres so that he could kiss her.

'Tell me your dress size and I'll arrange for an evening gown to be delivered to the villa.' Nico's voice deepened to a sexy drawl that sent a wave of anticipation across Sienna's skin. 'You won't need any other clothes because, aside from the party, I plan for you to be naked for the rest of the weekend.'

Of course she was going to refuse to go with him. 'I can only stay for one night,' Sienna heard herself say.

His wicked grin dismantled the last of her defences. 'In that case we had better make it a night to remember. I hope you don't expect to get any sleep.' Nico dipped his head and crushed her lips beneath his, kissing her with a devastating sensuality that left her trembling. She gave a moan of disappointment when he set her away from him.

'Rose and Iris are sitting in the orangery and might see us. We don't want them to think we are having a romance,' he said coolly.

His words were a reminder that she should not have any illusions about why he had invited her to his home in Italy, Sienna acknowledged. The sexual chemistry between them was explosive, but it would burn out and she was confident that she would walk away from him with her heart intact.

CHAPTER SIX

THEY FLEW TO Italy on Nico's private jet and a chauf-feured limousine was waiting at the airport to take them to the villa. Sienna remembered that when she had been Nico's wife she'd never grown used to her new, luxurious lifestyle.

Her lack of self-assurance had meant that she did not fit in with his wealthy social circle, and she'd been conscious of the rumours that she had married him for his money. Nothing could have been further from the truth. He had been her first love—her only love so far, she admitted wryly. As a teenager, she had been infatuated with him, and, caught up in the intensity of her own emotions, she had naively assumed that he felt the same way about her.

With a soft sigh, she turned her head and looked at Villa Lionard as it came into view. The De Conti's magnificent mansion, which Nico had inherited when his father died, stood on a peninsula on the shores of Lake Garda. The house was set in exquisitely landscaped grounds with uninterrupted views over the lake to the mountains beyond.

It was early evening and the sun was just lowering in the sky, bathing the lake in a golden light and dancing across the villa's large swimming pool. The mingled scents of lemon and olive groves that grew on either side of the driveway drifted in through the car's open windows. Nico was sitting beside Sienna and she felt him relax when the car stopped in front of the house. He had once told her that he regarded Villa Lionard as his true home. But although she could appreciate the beauty of the villa she had never felt that she belonged here, and she was beginning to question whether it had been a good idea to come back to the house that held painful memories for her.

They had spent their last Christmas together at the villa. It had been bitterly cold and the snow-covered mountains surrounding the lake had looked beautiful, but Sienna had barely noticed the scenery. She'd been desperately unhappy and her failure to fall pregnant again had put a strain on their marriage. A distance had grown between her and Nico, and he had seemed to withdraw from her even more after he'd visited his brother Danny in London, although he had denied that anything was wrong when she'd asked him.

She had hoped they could resolve their issues while they were in Italy, but, with the exception of Christmas Day, Nico had gone to his office in Verona every day and had often spent the night at his apartment in the city instead of driving back to the villa. He'd made the excuse of not wanting to drive in the snow, but she had been torn apart by jealousy, convinced that he was having an affair with his glamorous personal assistant, Rafaela Ferrante.

There was no point dredging up the past, Sienna told herself when Nico ushered her into the villa. She was a different person from the girl with a head full of dreams she had been years ago. He drew her into his arms and kissed her with a thoroughness that stirred the embers of her desire to fierce flames and drove every other thought from her mind except for her longing for him to take her to bed.

'I have a couple of calls to make,' he said when he finally stepped away from her, breathing hard. 'The maid will show you the dresses I ordered from a designer in Verona. I wasn't sure what style you would like, but my personal favourite is the black velvet.'

Nico had good taste, Sienna decided later, when she'd followed the maid into the dressing room of the master suite where a selection of dresses was hanging on a rail. The black velvet gown emphasised her narrow waist and the daringly low-cut neckline framed the creamy upper slopes of her breasts. Her pulse quickened as she wondered how he would react when he discovered that she was wearing the sheer stockings that had been left for her together with exquisite black lace underwear. A pair of high-heeled silver sandals gave her an extra four inches of height, and a silver clutch bag was the perfect accessory.

She had caught her hair up in a loose chignon and was wearing more make-up than usual. The dress was sexy yet sophisticated; the kind of dress a rich man's mistress would wear. Was that why Nico had picked it for her? She smoothed her hand over the curve of her hip, enjoying the feel of the sensuous material beneath her fingertips as she imagined Nico doing the same thing. She felt wickedly decadent. He wanted a mistress and she was happy to fulfil the role without hope or expectation that their relationship would develop outside the bedroom, she assured herself.

The hairs on the back of her neck prickled and she turned her head to see Nico enter the suite. He looked mouth-watering in a black tuxedo and snowy white shirt that contrasted with his olive-gold skin. When he strode into the dressing room he stopped abruptly and his blue eyes blazed with a sultry heat that caused Sienna's heart to skip a beat.

'You look incredible.' He slipped an arm around her waist and dipped his head to claim her mouth in a hungry kiss. Something feral tightened his features when she responded to him with an eagerness she did not try to hide. 'Have pity on me, *cara mia*,' he said thickly. 'I'm going to spend the evening fantasising about taking your dress off.'

The party was in the villa's huge reception room.

Nico introduced Sienna to the other guests and she was pleased by how much Italian she recalled from the lessons she had taken during her marriage. They had planned to bring up their baby to be bilingual, and she felt a familiar ache in her heart as she thought of her tiny son who had never lived.

'*Buonasera*, Sienna. I did not know that you would be here tonight.'

Sienna turned away from the window where she had been watching the moon glinting on the lake and her heart gave a jolt as she met the cool stare of Rafaela Ferrante. The Italian woman looked elegant in a white halter-neck dress, with her black hair falling in glossy waves around her shoulders.

'Rafaela. I wasn't expecting to see you, either. Are you still Nico's personal assistant?'

'Yes, but not for much longer.' Rafaela smiled. 'Nico has known for a long time what I want, and now at last my hopes are about to come true. I must go and speak with him. Excuse me, *per favore*.'

Sienna stared after Nico's PA, shaken by the realisation that Rafaela had played an important role in his life for the past eight years. She watched Nico greet Rafaela with a kiss on each cheek. It was a common continental greeting, but the intimacy evident between them evoked an acid burn in the pit of Sienna's stomach when the pair moved away to a quiet corner of the room, their dark heads close together while they were deep in conversation.

She was still wondering what Rafaela had meant when Nico returned to her a while later. 'Why are you frowning, *cara*?' he murmured as he swept her into his arms and onto the dance floor. She caught her breath when he pulled her close to him, helping to allay her old insecurities about his relationship with his beautiful secretary.

'I was wondering when the party will finish,' she said, skimming her hand over his shirt front and dragging her nails across one hard male nipple.

He swore and dropped his hand from her waist to the base of her spine, bringing her pelvis into sizzling contact with his. 'Soon, if there is a god,' he growled. 'See what you do to me, *bellissima*.'

'I can feel what I do to you,' she teased, moving her hips sinuously against him. She had never thought of herself as a seductress before, but Nico made her feel wild and free and very sexy.

'You know I will have to punish you later,' he warned, the gleam in his eyes sending a thrill of anticipation through her. He kept to his word when the last guests departed and he scooped her into his arms and carried her up to his bedroom. He set her down on her feet and unhooked her arms from around his neck. 'I am going to undress you,' he told her, his gravelly voice scraping across her nerve-endings, 'but you are not allowed to touch me until I say so.'

She pouted at him but could not restrain a shiver

of excitement when he stood behind her and ran the zip of her dress down her spine. He tugged the bodice down to her waist and slid his arms around her, cupping her bare breasts in his palms and rubbing her taut nipples between his fingers until she whimpered with pleasure. Sienna leaned back against his chest, watching their twin reflections in the mirror as Nico pressed his mouth to her white throat, trailed his lips up to her earlobe and then moved down to feather kisses along her collarbone.

'You are so goddamned beautiful,' he said in a harsh voice, as if he was struggling for control. In the mirror she saw his skin tighten over his sharp cheekbones. He reminded her of a wolf, dark and dangerous, and he had very sharp teeth, she discovered, catching her breath when he bit her neck.

He stripped the velvet dress from her body and tugged her lacy thong down her legs. But he left her stockings on when he pushed her down on the bed and put his mouth between her thighs to bestow an intimate caress with his wickedly inventive tongue that brought her to a shattering orgasm.

'You can touch me now,' he said, laughing at her eagerness as she tore at his shirt, sending buttons flying in her feverish haste to get her hands on his bare skin. She dealt with his trousers and boxers with the same urgency before she pushed him down on the mattress and straddled him. A grin lit his handsome face and made him even more gorgeous.

'You're amazing, *gattina*. Just watch what you are doing with your sharp, kitten claws.'

In a swift movement he reversed their positions and knelt over her, nudging her legs apart with his knee before he entered her with a deep thrust that drove the breath from her body. He made love to her again and again until they were both finally sated, and Sienna fell asleep with Nico's arms around her.

He was still holding her when she woke first the next morning. She lay quite still and studied him. While he slept his chiselled features were softer and reminded her poignantly of the boyishly handsome Nico she had married. A decade on, his face was all hard angles and planes, and his body was a powerhouse of taut muscles. She wondered how many lovers he'd had since they had divorced. Whatever the tally, it was a hundred per cent more than she'd had, but she certainly would not admit that to him.

With a soft sigh she started to ease away from him, but his arms tightened around her, and her heart missed a beat when she lifted her eyes to his face and found him watching her from beneath his thick black lashes. He gave her a lazy smile. 'Why the sigh, *cara*?'

'I'm hungry.' It was partly the truth, she acknowledged when her stomach growled. Thankfully the nauseous feeling she'd had for the past few mornings had gone and she put it down to a mild stomach upset.

'I may be able to do something about that,' Nico

drawled, throwing back the sheet to reveal his erection. He took her again with such mind-blowing sensuality that she wondered how she could possibly bring herself to leave him and go home. But she was due to leave in a few hours. Nico had arranged for her to be flown back to London on his private jet later in the afternoon and so far he hadn't mentioned a date in the future when they might meet again.

From the en-suite bathroom she heard the shower running, and molten warmth pooled between her legs as she pictured him standing beneath the spray, the water streaming over his muscular body. She was turning into a sex maniac, Sienna thought ruefully. More worrying was her emotional response to him. She would be a fool to fall in love with him, but when had love ever been sensible?

Her phone rang and, half asleep, she stretched out her hand to pick it up from the bedside table. But it was Nico's phone that was ringing and she realised they had the same ringtone as she stared at Rafaela's name on the screen before the phone went silent. Wide awake now, she rolled onto her back and frowned at the ceiling.

Why was Rafaela calling Nico so early? Could a work-related issue be so urgent that his PA needed to disturb him on a Sunday morning? She remembered Rafaela's curious statement at the party that her hopes were about to come true, and how Nico had spent ages talking to her. It was often said that the relationship between a boss and his personal assistant was as close as that between a husband and wife. That had been true in her own marriage, Sienna thought bleakly.

'You had a missed call,' she told Nico when he strolled out of the en-suite bathroom. He was wearing a towel tied around his hips and droplets of water glistened in his chest hair. He leaned over the bed and dropped a light kiss on her mouth. Before he could move away, she stroked her hand over his taut abdomen and slid her fingers beneath the edge of the towel. A part of her hated herself for wanting to keep his attention on her rather than on his phone.

'You are insatiable, *cara*,' he teased. He picked up his phone, glanced at the screen and straightened up. 'The household staff have Sundays off, so I'll go and make some coffee.'

When he walked out of the bedroom, Sienna heard his voice, low and intimate, as he headed along the corridor towards the stairs. Knowing that he was talking to Rafaela evoked a sharp stab of jealousy in her heart. She felt marginally better after she'd showered and dressed in her jeans and a silky top. Before she went to find Nico she carried her overnight case downstairs to the hall.

He was still talking on his phone and she hovered uncertainly in the kitchen doorway. He glanced over at her and murmured something in Italian into his phone that she did not catch before he ended the call.

'You didn't have to get up yet,' he said as he poured her a cup of coffee from the jug. 'We have a few hours until you fly back to London and it would be a shame to waste them.'

'Would it?' she said stiffly. 'I mistook your phone for mine and saw that it was Rafaela who called you. Perhaps you have other plans.' The minute she uttered the words she realised how childish she sounded, but it was too late to retract them.

Nico's eyes narrowed. 'Are you sulking because I spoke to my personal assistant?'

'I'm not sulking.' His arrogant tone made her temper simmer. She lifted her cup to her lips, but the strong aroma of coffee exacerbated the nauseous feeling that had swept over her when she'd got out of bed. Jealousy had unpleasant side-effects, she thought grimly. 'I admit I was surprised that your secretary phoned you at the weekend. Maybe I should have expected that you still have a close relationship with Rafaela. But you assured me that you aren't involved with anyone else.'

'So do you think I lied?' Nico's voice was cool. 'What exactly are you implying? Stop skirting around whatever it is that's bothering you and spit it out.'

She gritted her teeth. 'All right, I will. Do you have a personal relationship with Rafaela?'

His eyes narrowed on her flushed face. 'Is that really what you think? That after spending the night making love to you I raced out of bed to talk in secret to my mistress?' Nico gave her a scathing look. 'I thought you had grown up, Sienna, but clearly I was wrong. Your illogical suspicions were part of the reason we divorced.'

'It wasn't illogical to believe that you and Rafaela were lovers when I found her in your arms eight years ago,' she snapped.

She remembered how she had gone to the apartment in Verona, hoping to make up with him after their latest row. She hadn't told him she was coming and had used her key to let herself in. But when she'd walked into the lounge she had found Nico sitting on the sofa with his beautiful assistant. His arm had been around Rafaela's shoulders, and they had been deep in conversation. At her cry of distress they had sprung apart, looking guilty.

She stared at Nico across the kitchen counter. 'It would be ironic if you had been having an affair with Rafaela for the past eight years. Many marriages don't last that long. Ours certainly didn't.'

'But Rafaela's marriage is still going strong, and she and her husband recently celebrated their tenth wedding anniversary.'

Shocked, Sienna stared at him. 'Rafaela is married?'

Nico nodded. 'Soon after their marriage her husband had a car accident, which left him partially paralysed. Rafaela was distraught when Claudio wanted to divorce her so that she could meet someone else. She confided in me because she couldn't talk to her family. Fortunately she managed to convince Claudio that he is the love of her life. Last night she told me that their application to adopt a baby boy has been accepted, and she intends to give up work and devote herself to being a mother. Her call this morning was to update me with the news that she and Claudio will take their new son home next week.'

'Why didn't you tell me about Rafaela's problems when we had problems with our own marriage?' Sienna bit her lip. 'You knew I suspected that you were involved with her but you didn't deny there was anything going on between you.'

'I shouldn't have had to deny it,' he said harshly. 'You should have trusted me. I had never given you reason to doubt my commitment to our marriage.'

'A marriage you didn't want.' Her voice shook with the emotions she could no longer contain. 'I loved you, but you married me out of duty because I was pregnant, didn't you, Nico?'

He shrugged. 'Perhaps.'

His reply felt like a knife in her heart, and with a flash of insight Sienna understood that his relationship with his PA had not been the real issue with their marriage. She had convinced herself that Nico was having an affair with Rafaela rather than acknowledge that his coolness and the way he kept an emotional distance from her were because he did not love her and he felt trapped in their marriage that he hadn't wanted. With painful honesty she realised that she had been kidding herself to think that she could have a sex-without-strings affair with him. It wasn't enough for her. But Nico had made it clear that he would not offer more, certainly not his heart.

He drained his coffee and set his cup down on the counter so hard that she was surprised the china didn't smash. 'I'll go and put some clothes on, and then we'll have some breakfast. Perhaps your mood will improve after you've eaten,' he said sardonically.

Sienna's stomach churned at the mere thought of food. Worse was the shameful throb of desire between her legs when his half-naked body brushed against her as he walked past. No, she corrected herself. *Worse* was the temptation she felt to follow him upstairs to the bedroom and make love with him again. He was like a drug in her system but the longer she stayed with him, the harder it would be to break her addiction. A clean break was necessary.

She waited in the kitchen until she heard the slam of the bedroom door upstairs, and then she grabbed her holdall from the hall and raced out of the villa, searching on her phone for the number of a local taxi company. As she hurried down the driveway towards the main gates she promised herself that this time she was leaving Nico for good.

CHAPTER SEVEN

NICO SLAMMED HIS fists into the punchbag; right fist, left fist, again and again until his arms and shoulders ached. Finally he pulled off his boxing gloves and threw them onto the floor of Villa Lionard's well-equipped gym. His jaw clenched. It seemed that not even hard physical exercise could prevent his thoughts from turning to Sienna after she had walked out on him *again*. The third time she had done so.

It was two months since they had argued and he'd watched her from the bedroom window climbing into a taxi. He had told himself that he was well rid of her. It had been a mistake to get involved with her again and he'd vowed to forget about her. But she was on his mind constantly. He had pulled her number up on his phone countless times but his pride had stopped him from calling her.

He assured himself that what he missed was the amazing sex. But the thought niggled that if it was only physical satisfaction he wanted he could find a release for his urges easily enough. He'd never had a problem attracting women. The problem was that the only woman he wanted had an annoying habit of leaving him.

He told himself that he didn't give a damn. But deep down he felt a gut-wrenching ache of rejection; the same feeling he'd had when he was a boy and his mother had tried to take her own life. There must be something wrong with him that his mother would have preferred death to staying alive to care for her sons, he'd reasoned. That was why he had always looked after Danny and tried to be a parent to him, after their own parents had, in one way or another, abandoned their children.

Cursing beneath his breath, Nico shoved his emotions back into the box where he had locked them away since he was twelve years old. His life functioned perfectly well without messy feelings and without his ex-wife, he assured himself.

His phone rang, and his expression softened when he saw the name of the caller. '*Buongiorno*, Nonna. What's the weather like in Yorkshire?'

'Domenico, have you seen the news reports?' Iris sounded anxious. 'There has been a coup in Tutjo and the King has been deposed. Civil war has broken out and the situation there looks terrible. I've just had Rose Fisher on the phone. She is desperately worried because Sienna flew to Tutjo a few days ago.'

Nico frowned. 'I told Sienna not to travel to that area of Africa. Trouble has been brewing on and off in Tutjo for months.'

'I don't think Sienna would react well to being told what to do, or not do,' his grandmother said thoughtfully. 'I admire her independent spirit.'

'Let's hope it hasn't got her into serious trouble,' Nico muttered, using the remote to switch the TV onto the news channel. The pictures of the escalating violence in Tutjo were horrifying. Sienna wasn't his responsibility, he reminded himself. But the lump of fear that dropped like a lead weight into the pit of his stomach mocked his belief that she meant nothing to him.

Sienna fanned her hot face with her hand. The tiny room where she was confined did not have air conditioning and the window was locked the same as the door. The heat was stifling. When the men who had brought her here at gunpoint came back, perhaps they would bring her some water.

Fear gripped her when she looked out of the window at the main street of Assana, the capital city of the small African state of Tutjo. Burning tyres, shattered glass from shop windows, burnt-out trucks and gangs of men carrying guns were signs of a violent uprising by rebels opposed to the King. The coup had started two days after she had arrived in Tutjo. There had been no warning on the UK government's

Foreign Office website that it was unsafe to travel to the region, and her brother-in-law in nearby South Africa had assured her that the recent tensions in Tutjo had calmed down.

She hugged her arms around her, trying to quell her panic as she wondered what would happen to her now that Tutjo was a lawless state. Yesterday she should have gone to meet the women from the cooperative that supplied her with Marula oil, and she hoped that they were all safe.

The door suddenly opened and Sienna spun round and stared at the armed man who entered the room. He pointed his gun at her, and her heart thudded with fear when he spoke in a heavy accent. 'You, come.'

Maybe the rebels were going to let her go free, she told herself as she walked along a corridor. But if that was so, why was she being threatened with a rifle in her back? When she had been seized from her hotel, one of her captors who spoke a little English had told her that they suspected she was a foreign journalist working for the deposed King.

'In here.' The gunman opened a door and pushed her into a room. There were four or five men gathered around a desk, but Sienna's gaze flew to the man standing apart from the others.

'Nico!'

He strode towards her and caught her as she hurtled into his arms. 'Are you all right?' He slid a hand under her chin and tipped her face up to his, swearing softly when he saw tears in her eyes. 'If the men have harmed you in any way…'

'I'm fine,' she reassured him. She sagged against his whipcord body, feeling weak with relief and shock at seeing him again. The evocative scent of his aftershave was like a homecoming. She was conscious that her cotton trousers and shirt were crumpled, and strands of hair had escaped her ponytail and were sticking to her hot face. Nico wore faded jeans that hugged his lean hips and a denim shirt with the sleeves rolled up to his elbows. The dark stubble on his jaw was an indication that he hadn't shaved for a couple of days and he looked sexier than ever. 'How did you know where I was?' Sienna asked him shakily.

'Your brother-in-law knew which hotel you were staying at. Most of the staff who worked there had gone, but I found someone who had seen you being taken away by the gunmen, and I discovered that this office block is the rebels' headquarters.'

'I'm so worried about the women who work for the cooperatives and their families.'

An odd expression crossed his face. 'You are something else, *cara*. Captured by gunmen but your concern is for others rather than yourself.' He smoothed her hair off her face, but the man who had brought Sienna to the room grabbed hold of her arm and pulled her away from Nico.

'If you want your woman you must pay for her.'

'What did he mean?' she whispered when Nico threw the bag he was holding down on the desk.

'I've been trying to negotiate your release.'

Her fear turned to anger as she looked around at the men who were all brandishing weapons even though they knew that she was unarmed. They were pathetic bullies. 'Have the rebels demanded money? How much do they want?'

'One million US dollars,' Nico told her in a low tone, his eyes on the gunmen.

'That's outrageous…' The rest of her angry words were muffled beneath Nico's lips as his head swooped down and he captured her mouth in a hard kiss. 'What are you doing?' she muttered when he allowed her to draw a breath.

'Saving your life and probably mine. These guys aren't carrying toy guns.' His eyes glittered with a warning and she felt guilty thinking that he had risked his life by coming to Tutjo to rescue her. The situation was highly dangerous and the best thing she could do was allow Nico to deal with the rebels.

He spoke with the man who seemed to be the leader of the gunmen, but the voices washed over Sienna as she fought another bout of dizziness that had plagued her even before she had come to Africa. She had mentioned that she'd been experiencing dizzy spells to a nurse friend who had suggested that she could be anaemic. When she got home—*if* she got home—she would make an appointment with her GP and ask for a blood test.

Nico handed the backpack over to one of the men who proceeded to take out wads of dollar bills and count them. Finally the man seemed satisfied and threw Sienna's passport down on the desk.

'They're letting us go,' Nico murmured in her ear. She swayed on her feet and was grateful for the arm he clamped around her waist as he strode out of the room with her. 'Keep on walking. There's a truck waiting outside for us.'

The journey through rebel-held Tutjo to neighbouring South Africa was tense, and Sienna only relaxed when they were aboard Nico's jet and it took off from the runway. She hadn't slept since her capture, and she did not argue when Nico showed her to the bedroom on the plane and suggested she get some rest. She was asleep as soon as her head was on the pillow and barely stirred when the jet landed and she was carried to a car.

'Are we in London?' she asked when she opened her eyes and looked out at dark, unfamiliar streets.

'Italy. We'll arrive at Villa Lionard in a few minutes,' Nico told her.

'I thought you were taking me back to my flat.' She flushed when she realised that she had been sleeping with her head on his shoulder, and quickly sat upright.

His eyes gleamed in the dark car. 'We have unfinished business from the last time you were at the villa.'

Sienna bit her lip, remembering her stupid accusation that he was having an affair with his secretary. 'I'm sorry I suggested that you were sleeping with Rafaela,' she muttered.

The car came to a halt and Nico sprang out and scooped her off the back seat into his arms. 'The only woman I want to sleep with is you, *mia bellezza.*' He looked down at her, and his wolfish expression was accentuated by his grin that revealed his white teeth.

She had promised herself that she wouldn't do this again. But how could she resist him, she thought despairingly, when his arms were like bands of steel around her and he was holding her against the solid wall of his chest, against his heart? She felt safe, which was crazy, because Nico—or rather her reaction to him—was a danger she knew she should avoid at all cost. Yet he had rescued her from the rebels in Tutjo and in all likelihood he'd saved her life.

He carried her upstairs and into the master bedroom, setting her on her feet in the en-suite bathroom. His fingers deftly unfastened the buttons on her shirt and she caught her breath when his knuckles brushed against the side of her breast as he removed her bra.

'I can take a shower on my own. I'm not a child.'

'I have yet to be convinced of that,' he told her

sardonically. 'You disobeyed me after I warned you against going to Tutjo.'

'Disobeyed?' she choked. 'You are so arrogant, Nico. I don't have to obey you. You don't own me.'

'As a matter of fact, I do.' He tugged her trousers down her legs, followed by her panties and lifted her into the shower cubicle before he turned on the spray. 'I paid one million dollars for you.'

The water from the shower cascaded over her face and hair, washing away the grime and fear of the past days and making her skin tingle. Excitement heated her blood as she watched him strip off his clothes before he stepped into the cubicle with her. She lifted her hands to his chest, but instead of pushing him away as her brain told her to do, she ran her fingers through the dark hair that arrowed down his torso. She'd missed him. *Missed* him so badly. 'Do you expect me to have sex with you to repay the debt I owe you? I thought you were a gentleman.'

Nico laughed. 'I'm afraid I am not, *cara*.' He splayed his hands over her breasts, bringing her nipples to stinging life when he rolled them between his fingers. 'How many nights in my bed do you think it will take to work off a million dollars?' He captured her chin and tilted her face up to his. The amusement in his eyes was replaced with an emotion Sienna could not define but which made her heart lurch. 'I thought I'd lost you,' he said roughly before he brought his mouth down on hers and kissed her with an urgency that simply destroyed her.

She parted her lips to the fierce demands of his and kissed him back with mounting passion, wild and hot, her hands moving over his body, exploring the hard ridges of his abdominal muscles, sliding round to his back and down to his taut buttocks. He felt divine: satin skin, hair-roughened thighs and his shaft was steel encased in velvet as he hardened to her touch.

He muttered her name, and then his mouth was on her breast, his lips closing around the nipple, and sucking hard until the pleasure was too intense and she cried out. Her fingers gripped his hair as he moved across to her other breast and wrought havoc with his tongue, while he slipped his hand between her legs and found the slick heat of her arousal with one probing finger and then two.

'Wrap your legs around me,' he growled as he lifted her, cupping her bottom cheeks and settling her against him so that his erection was there at her opening. And then he simply drove his hard length into her, taking her breath away with the mastery of his possession. She gloried in his fierce desire for her, in his harsh groans as she welcomed each bold thrust, tilting her hips so that he could go deeper.

Nico paused for a moment and rested his forehead against hers, his chest heaving. 'I'm going to come,' he said harshly. 'You always make me lose control.'

He sounded almost angry, but Sienna could only concentrate on the coiling sensation inside her that was pulling tighter and tighter. She was lost to this man, only this man. He began to move again, his hands gripping her hips, his eyes closed as he pumped in and out, faster and faster, taking them both higher until she screamed his name and tumbled into the mindless, indescribable pleasure of her orgasm.

He tensed, and she sensed he was trying to hold back the tide. His eyes glittered beneath the sweep of his thick black lashes. *'Tesoro mio,'* he muttered, before he drove into her one more time, his face pressed against her throat so that when he exploded inside her she felt his triumphant shout ricochet through her.

A long time later, after he had taken her to bed and made love to her with an inventiveness that had her on her knees, her face buried in the pillows while he positioned himself behind her, Sienna hovered on the edge of sleep and remembered that the English translation of *tesoro mio* was *my treasure*. Dared she hope that he meant it?

Dio! What a night! Nico stretched luxuriously. The pale light of early morning filtered through the blinds, and he rolled onto his side, propping himself up on his elbow so that he could study Sienna, still asleep beside him. Her dark red hair streamed like ribbons of silk over the pillows and her eyelashes made crescents on her cheeks.

His beautiful English rose. Something moved inside him, a possessiveness he wanted to reject. Frowning, he shifted onto his back and stared up at the ceiling. The chemistry between them had always been off the scale but he knew better than to look for a deeper meaning that might explain why he had slept with one arm clamped across her waist to prevent her from leaving him in the middle of the night.

'Thank you for rescuing me from the rebels.'

He turned his head and looked into her smoke-soft grey eyes. The hint of vulnerability on her lovely face got to him more than he was comfortable with. 'It was my pleasure,' he murmured, feeling his heart kick in his chest when he drew her unresisting body towards him. He had taken his pleasure with her several times last night and he was as hard as a spike again. Stranger to understand was the sense of completeness he felt every time he had sex with Sienna. What he felt for her *was* only physical attraction, he assured himself. But he wasn't ready to let her go—yet.

Her mouth opened like the petals of a flower when he kissed her, but she pushed against his shoulder as he moved over her. 'I need to go to the bathroom first.'

Reluctantly he released her so that she could swing her legs over the side of the bed. But when she stood up, the colour drained from her face and she gave a low cry. Nico realised that she was about to faint, and he threw himself across the bed, just managing to catch her as her legs crumpled beneath her.

'It was probably a reaction to the stress I was under in Tutjo,' she argued a few minutes later, after he had put her back into bed. 'There was no need for you to call a doctor.'

'Nevertheless *il dottore*—Dr Belucci—will be here soon to check you over. He is an old family friend and lives not far from the villa.' He kissed away her pout. 'Don't sulk, *cara*. Perhaps there is a simple reason why you fainted but I want to be sure.'

Stefano Belucci had been a physician to the De Conti family since before Nico was born. When the maid ushered the doctor into the bedroom, Nico glanced at Sienna. 'Do you want me to leave the room, *cara*?'

She shrugged. 'Stay if you want to.'

Sienna answered all the doctor's questions about her general health. 'There's nothing wrong with me,' she insisted.

'I will take some blood and urine samples, Signorina Fisher. There are a number of reasons which could explain the dizziness that you say you have experienced recently.'

Nico moved over to the window while Dr Belucci performed various tasks, and then Sienna went into the bathroom and returned soon after and handed the doctor a small container. She was still pale, and her air of fragility made Nico feel guilty that he had been too demanding last night. Her passion had matched his, he reminded himself, but inexplicably he felt a need to protect her.

'When will you have the results of the blood tests?' he asked the doctor.

'In a day or two. But I am confident that I know the cause of Signorina Fisher's symptoms.' Dr Belucci looked from Nico to Sienna, and smiled. '*Congratulazioni!* You are pregnant.'

CHAPTER EIGHT

How was he in this situation again? Toxic anger surged through Nico's veins. The realisation that Sienna must be laughing at him made him want to punch the wall of the study where he had come after the doctor had made his astonishing announcement.

She was pregnant! His lying, cheating ex-wife had played him for a fool once again. And the worst of it was she was so goddamned clever that he had almost been taken in by her shocked expression. He had almost been convinced that she hadn't planned this all along.

'I can't believe it,' she'd whispered, and the stunned look in her wide, grey eyes had been a touching performance worthy of a standing ovation. Nico had walked out of the room then, and ignored her when she'd called after him, but her soft voice had cut like a jagged knife blade through his soul. She was pregnant but it wasn't his child.

He welcomed his fury that burned as hot as the fires of hell in his gut. It released him from the spell she had cast on him when he'd glanced over his shoulder in the church at Danny's wedding and seen a vision of loveliness in a yellow dress. But now he felt nothing but contempt for her.

'Nico.'

He tensed and jerked his head round to see her standing in the doorway. If anything she looked even paler than she had when she'd fainted, and the slight tremble of her lips before she pressed them firmly together should not have tugged on his heart. It didn't, he told himself.

'The news is incredible, isn't it?' she murmured as she walked into the study and closed the door. 'I'm still in shock. But Dr Belucci is one hundred per cent certain that I am going to have a baby.'

'I'm not sure what you want me to say,' he bit out. 'Do you want me to offer you my congratulations? Out of curiosity, is the father someone you were involved with before you slept with me on a number of occasions, or did you meet your lover after you stormed out of the villa two months ago?'

'You don't understand.' The stricken look on her face was a masterpiece of acting, he thought sardonically. 'I am expecting your baby, Nico. The pregnancy test showed that I am approximately fourteen weeks pregnant which means that I must have conceived in June. We made love after Danny's wedding,' she reminded him, and then he understood.

'I wondered why you had turned up at the church.

And then there was the story you spun about Iris having an angina attack, which was patently an excuse for you to visit my bedroom. You were keen to have sex with me that night so that you could name me as the father of the child you were already carrying. Very clever, *cara*,' he said mockingly. 'But I am not so stupid as to fall for the same trick twice.'

Sienna made a soft sound of distress, and Nico tore his eyes from her, fighting an inexplicable urge to take her in his arms. Her lush body with those firm, round breasts acted like a siren's song and he despised himself because, even now, knowing what she was, he still ached to touch her.

'What do you mean? I've never tried to trick you.' Her voice was a thread of sound but she lifted her chin and said in a firmer tone, 'This baby is most definitely yours because you are the only man I've ever had sex with.' She bit her lip when he gave a snort of derision. 'It's the truth. Why would I pretend that you are the father of my child?'

'For the same reason that you fooled me into believing I was responsible for your first pregnancy. I am very wealthy.' He shrugged. 'And perhaps you fancy yourself as a viscountess. You really are a very good actress. I could almost be taken in by you. But the baby you are carrying cannot be mine because I am infertile.'

'But…you can't be.' She swayed on her feet, and the memory of how he had caught her just before she'd collapsed onto the bedroom floor when she'd fainted earlier caused Nico to swear.

'Sit down,' he said roughly. He steered her over to the sofa, his jaw clenching when she leaned her head back against the cushions. How dared she look so vulnerable when he knew it was an act?

'Why do you think you are infertile?' Sienna sounded as weary as Nico felt. He was tired of lies, tired of wishing for something that he did not fully understand and had decided a long time ago that he did not want. At a young age, his parents' volatile marriage had taught him that emotions and relationships were a combination doomed to failure.

'I did a test which showed that I have a low sperm count,' he said curtly. 'We had been trying for a year to have another baby and it seemed odd that you didn't conceive, especially considering that you had fallen pregnant the first time we'd slept together.' He exhaled heavily. 'You were obsessed with ovulation charts and sex had become a means to an end. It seemed as though you only wanted to make love if there was a chance you would get pregnant. Every month when I found you crying, I felt a failure.'

'I felt a failure too,' she said quietly. 'I had miscarried your heir and I couldn't give you another child.'

'But Luigi wasn't mine.' Nico ignored her gasp, reminding himself again that Sienna was a clever actress. Maybe everything she did was an act, and her husky moans when he'd held back from taking his own pleasure so that he could give her multiple orgasms had been as fake as her claim that he was her only lover. 'I know that you slept with my brother before we became lovers ten years ago.'

She blinked. 'With *Danny*?'

'I only have one brother,' he drawled.

Colour flared on her white face. 'I didn't sleep with him or anyone else. I *was* a virgin when I made love with you.' She pushed her hair back from her face. 'Where did you get the crazy idea that I had slept with Danny?'

'He admitted that you'd had sex with him only a few days before I arrived at Sethbury Hall,' Nico said abruptly. 'When we met, you immediately dropped Danny and turned your interest on me, I assume because you knew I would inherit the estate and peerage.'

'It's not true. I went on a couple of dates with Danny before you came to Much Matcham. I suppose I knew that he wanted to take our relationship a step further. I liked him as a friend but I wasn't in love with him and nothing happened between us.'

Nico's jaw clenched. 'Danny is my kid brother and I've looked out for him since he was a toddler. He and I have always been close. Best friends as well as brothers.'

'Danny was jealous of you. He said that you were the heir and he was the spare. I was never his,' Sienna said in a fierce voice that added fuel to Nico's fury because she was such a damned good liar.

'I don't believe my brother would lie to me. I suppose it's possible that you did not know which of us—Danny or me—was the father of your child, but you were in love with me and so you let me think it was my baby, knowing that I would be duty-bound to marry the mother of my heir,' he told her brutally.

Sienna hunched forwards and covered her face with her hands. 'Luigi was yours,' she whispered. She lowered her hands and stared at him. 'Maybe the result of the fertility test was wrong. It must have been, because I am expecting your baby now. But if you believed you were infertile when we tried to have a child why didn't you tell me? I thought it was my fault.'

Guilt stirred uncomfortably inside Nico. He hadn't mentioned the sperm test and its devastating result because he'd been embarrassed. It had felt like a slur on his masculinity, especially when he'd realised that his brother must have been responsible for Sienna's first pregnancy. 'We got divorced and I assumed you would meet someone else and have a child,' he said gruffly.

He looked away from her hurt expression, infuriated by the dull ache that had lodged beneath his breastbone. This was why he avoided emotions, he thought grimly. Sienna was a treacherous bitch and he had every right to evict her from his life without feeling as if he was the monster in a ridiculous melodrama.

He leaned his hip against the desk and folded his arms across his chest, his mouth twisting into a contemptuous smile when he saw the shimmer of tears in her eyes. 'So you see, Sienna, why I am certain that your pregnancy is not my concern. And why I want you to get out of my house and stay out of my life. I never want to set eyes on you for as long as I live,' he finished savagely.

'Don't worry, Nico. You will never see me again or meet your baby.' Sienna stood up and walked over to the door. Her eyes ached with the effort of holding back her tears, but she was determined not to let him see her cry. He had humiliated her enough and hurt her so badly with his vile accusations that she could never forgive him.

She did not have the energy to try to defend herself, and what was the point? Nico believed the lie his brother had told him and he refused to believe that he was the father of her baby. She was still struggling to absorb the news of her pregnancy. She hadn't noticed any signs, although she realised now it would explain her bouts of nausea and other odd symptoms. Her periods were sometimes light or irregular, and her mind had been on other things recently—mostly on Nico—so that she hadn't noticed her cycle was very late.

Nico's stunned expression when the doctor had made his announcement had reflected her own shocked disbelief, but when he'd walked out of the bedroom without saying anything, or even looking at her, she'd guessed he didn't share her joy. Maybe he just needed time to get used to the idea, she'd told herself as she'd quickly pulled on some clothes and gone after him. He might be angry at first but he would calm down and realise how lucky they were to finally be expecting a child together. The contempt in his voice when he'd told her to get out of his life had shattered her fragile hope that he would want her and his baby.

She resisted the urge to glance back at him as she walked out of the study. In the hall she found the chauffeur was waiting by the front door. He was holding the backpack that she'd brought with her from Tutjo. Head held high, she followed the chauffeur out of the villa, and when he opened the car door she climbed inside. She had no idea if Nico watched them drive away and told herself she didn't care. It was over.

His private jet landed in London a few hours later. She supposed she should be grateful that he had arranged for her to be flown home, instead of having to catch a commercial flight. A taxi delivered her to her flat in Camden and she went straight to her bedroom. Unable to hold back the storm of emotions that had been building since Nico had evicted her from his life, she threw herself down on the bed and cried until she could cry no more.

'It's just you and me, baby,' she whispered. Resting her hand on her stomach, she felt a faint but discernible swell—not a sign that she needed to hit the gym and tone up her stomach muscles as she'd thought, but evidence of a new life developing inside her. Through her misery came a gleam of light and a faint smile tugged at her lips. She sat up and wiped away her tears. Tomorrow she would make an appointment with her GP, and she knew from friends who'd had children that in the next couple of weeks she would be offered an ultrasound scan.

The pregnancy test that the doctor in Italy had carried out suggested that she was already past the crucial first three months. But her first pregnancy had ended at twenty-two weeks and she was scared to look too far into the future. All she could do was hope for the best. And she needed to look after herself, starting with eating properly, Sienna decided as she slid off the bed and went to the kitchen to cook herself some dinner. Nico had made it clear he did not want to be involved with the baby but they would manage just fine without him.

Nico emerged from a private clinic in Harley Street and climbed into the limousine that was parked beside the pavement. After instructing his driver to take him to an address in Maida Vale he leaned his head against the back of the seat and tried to make sense of the results he'd received, following tests he'd undergone to check his fertility.

'Everything is absolutely normal,' the specialist at the clinic had told him. 'It's possible that the test you did previously was flawed. Home fertility tests have improved in recent years, but the ones available in the past were unreliable and did not always give an accurate result.'

It was too late now to wish that he had discussed his concerns with a doctor and been tested properly years ago, Nico thought heavily. He had been much younger then, and a mix of immaturity and hurt pride had made him jump to the conclusion that Sienna had conceived his brother's baby after Danny had said that they had been lovers.

Although Nico had now discovered that it was perfectly feasible for him to be able to father a child, it did not automatically mean that he was responsible for Sienna's current pregnancy, he reminded himself. But her insistence that the result of the fertility test from years ago must have been wrong had led to his decision to be re-tested. He'd assumed that the latest result would confirm he was infertile and prove once and for all that Sienna was a liar. But that hadn't happened, and for the first time in his life Nico felt uncertain how to proceed.

She had looked so shocked when he'd accused her of sleeping with his brother. In the heat of his temper he'd believed she was a clever actress. But her denial had been so fierce, *so convincing*, that he'd started to wonder if she had told him the truth—which would mean that his brother had lied to him.

Nico raked his hand through his hair. He would trust Danny with his life. But the memory of Sienna's unhappy face haunted him. He knew he had been unnecessarily cruel when he'd sent her away. What if he had been wrong about her and the child was his? His jaw clenched as he remembered her parting words to him. 'You will never…meet your baby.'

Dio! He needed to have a conversation with his brother urgently.

Danny's penthouse flat was close to De Conti Leisure's London head office. Nico had created the role of Assistant to the Director of PR for his brother, but the reality was that Danny only worked when it suited him and he enjoyed a busy social life funded by the generous trust fund Nico had established for him. Sometimes the traitorous thought had crossed Nico's mind that his brother was as selfish as their mother. But Danny had been just a kid when their parents had divorced and Nico had always tried to shield him from life's upsets.

'What brings you to London?' Danny asked when he invited Nico into the penthouse and offered him a beer. 'Are you meeting Sienna? I admit I was surprised when Nonna told me that you'd invited your ex-wife to Sethbury Hall for lunch. I didn't think it was your style to resurrect an old relationship.'

'Would it bother you if I was seeing Sienna again?'

'Of course not. Why should it?' Danny suddenly seemed keen to avoid Nico's gaze.

'She denies that the two of you slept together ten years ago. So what is the truth?'

'For God's sake, why does it matter now?'

'It doesn't matter. I was merely curious,' Nico said in a deliberately bland voice.

'Oh, well.' Danny gave a shrug. 'I admit that I wasn't entirely truthful when I told you I'd slept with Sienna.'

Nico felt his stomach hit the floor. Hard on the heels of his shock at his brother's betrayal came the realisation that he had been terribly wrong about Sienna. *Madre di Dio!* She hadn't lied to him and it was possible, probable, he amended, remembering how she had insisted that he was the only man she'd had sex with—*in eight years*—that she was expecting his baby.

'Why did you lie to me?' he asked Danny in a low voice, trying to control his anger, trying even now to protect his brother, he thought bitterly. He felt gutted by Danny's deceit, which had cost him his marriage. But the unpalatable truth was that he couldn't blame anyone but himself, Nico acknowledged. His lack of trust had come between him and Sienna eight years ago and driven a wedge between them now.

'I knew you would hate the idea that I'd had Sienna first,' Danny muttered. 'You had everything, Nico. You were the heir and I was the afterthought. I really liked Sienna but the minute you showed up I might as well not have existed. You never cared that girls always fell in love with you. But it was different with Sienna. You were in love with her.'

Nico said nothing. He finished his beer and crushed the can in his fist. After a moment, Danny continued bitterly, 'I realised that Sienna was your weakness. I know it was a stupid thing to do, but when I told you that she'd been with me first it felt good knowing that you were envious of me for once. You had the money and the title and the power, but I'd had your girl. Except that really I hadn't. Sienna was madly in love with you. Surely you asked her for the truth while you were married to her? She would have denied sleeping with me.'

'I trusted you,' Nico said grittily. 'You are my kid brother and I thought there was a bond between us. I believed you.' The sense of betrayal he felt evoked a burning sensation behind his eyelids and he pinched the bridge of his nose while he attempted to marshal his thoughts. In his mind he pictured Sienna with tears in her eyes when he'd told her to stay out of his life.

What the hell had he done?

He'd heard nothing from her in the past three weeks. Surely if the child she was carrying was his, he would have received some sort of communication from her lawyers by now? But there had been nothing, no paternity claim—which might be because Sienna had slept with another man earlier in the summer and knew that she was pregnant with her lover's baby.

He had to know the truth. And if she *was* expecting his baby he *would* claim his heir. No way would he be as irresponsible as his father, he vowed grimly. Franco De Conti had fathered several illegitimate children and cut them out of his life. Nico had inherited his grandfather Rupert Mandeville's strong sense of duty, and, although he had loved his father, he had lost respect for him.

Sienna's business operated from a workshop beside the Regent's Canal in Camden. The door was unlocked, and when Nico walked in he found the desk in the small reception area was unmanned. It was early evening and he guessed that most of the staff had gone home. But when he pushed open the door into the workshop, he saw three people standing at a counter where there was an array of bottles and jars. At another time he would have been interested in the Victorian building with its redbrick walls, vaulted ceiling and exposed wooden beams. But his eyes were riveted on Sienna and he felt a painful sensation in his chest as though his heart had been squeezed in a vice.

She was so beautiful. He had committed every one of her features to his memory but he had forgotten the impact she always had on him, the way his breath felt as if it were trapped in his lungs when he stared at her lovely face. He skimmed his eyes over her, searching for signs of her pregnancy. But she looked slim in close-fitting black trousers tucked into knee-high black boots, and a loose white jumper that slipped down to reveal one bare shoulder.

Nico froze as it occurred to him that there might not be a baby. Sienna had suffered a miscarriage in her first pregnancy. *Dio!* He was only just coming to terms with the idea that she had conceived his child and he couldn't grasp that she might have lost it.

For a heartbeat Sienna could not hide her shock when her gaze met his, but she quickly schooled her expression to one of utter indifference that made Nico grind his teeth, even though he accepted that he deserved for her to look at him as if he were something unpleasant she had trodden in.

The two women with Sienna looked up as he walked across the workshop but they carried on packing jars of what he guessed was skin cream into boxes. Sienna glared at him fiercely as if she hoped he would get the message that he was unwelcome. But Nico wasn't going anywhere until he had an answer to the question that was eating away at him.

She glanced at her watch and spoke to the women. 'Carley and Liz, you can go now and I'll finish up here. Thanks for staying late. The courier will collect the order first thing in the morning.'

When the women had left the workshop she looked directly at Nico. He noted how her breasts rose quickly as she took a deep breath, and the idea that she was nervous gave another squeeze on his heart.

'I have no idea why you are here and I want you to leave,' she said coldly.

'We need to talk.'

'Really?' Her voice dripped with sarcasm. 'I can't say I feel the need to talk to you, Nico. The last time we met I distinctly remember you saying that you never wanted to see me again.'

She had not mentioned the baby. He stared at her, noting the faint purple smudges beneath her eyes, which suggested that her sleep had been as disturbed as his. 'Should you be working this late in the evening in your condition?' he growled.

'As if you care.' Her bitterness hit Nico like a punch in his gut and his jaw clenched when she continued in a hard voice that he had never heard her use before. 'You made your feelings for me and your child absolutely clear.'

So there was still a child. Relief and a host of other emotions he did not care to define roughened his voice when he said, 'I know now that Danny lied. When I confronted him he admitted he'd made up the story that you and he had been lovers. You

were right, he was jealous and wanted to hurt me.'
It scraped a raw place inside Nico to know that his
brother had resented him.

'It took you three weeks to get around to asking
your brother for the truth. I'm surprised you bothered
at all.' She gave him a scathing look that would have
felled other men less determined than Nico. He was
taken aback by Sienna's fury. Perhaps he should have
expected her anger but the teenager he'd married ten
years ago had been sweetly anxious to please him.
He had assumed he would be able to win her round
easily, he acknowledged ruefully. Clearly that was
not going to happen.

The woman watching him suspiciously was a li-
oness protecting her cub. She moved her hand over
her stomach and the instinctive gesture of maternal
devotion for her unborn baby crucified him when he
remembered how he had rejected her and his child.
Both his children, he was reminded when she spoke.

'How could you have believed that Luigi wasn't
your son? The poor little boy was denied a life and
denied his father's love. I will never forgive you for
that.'

Nico doubted he would ever forgive himself. He
had never told anyone that after they had lost Luigi
he had often visited his son's grave at night, and
alone in the darkness he had given in to the grief that
was a permanent ache in his heart. Nico had been
filled with regret that he hadn't been more enthusi-

astic when Sienna had announced she was pregnant. He'd been unprepared for fatherhood, but over time he'd begun to feel excited and it had been a savage blow when the baby had been stillborn. Later, when he'd believed that Luigi had not been his child, he'd stopped visiting the churchyard.

But right now was not the time to tell Sienna how much he regretted his past mistakes. He needed to convince her that he was here to put right the mistake he'd made when he had sent her away from Villa Lionard.

'I know Luigi was mine and I am prepared to believe that I am the father of the baby you are expecting.'

'How good of you,' she said scornfully. 'Although prepared to believe suggests you would want it confirmed by a paternity test.' She gave a hollow laugh as if she'd guessed that he had considered asking for a DNA test to be certain. But that had been before he'd seen her again and realised that, among other complicated things, he trusted her completely.

'Here's some news, Nico. I don't care whether you think this baby is yours or not. You will never have any involvement in his life.'

'His?' he said roughly, struggling to control the emotions that swept like a raging river through him. 'You are expecting my son?'

She tensed when he strode around the counter and halted in front of her. 'Yes, I'm having a boy,' she muttered. 'But you told me you are infertile, so he can't be your son. I must have fallen pregnant by one of my legions of lovers.' This time her sarcasm did not quite mask the quiver of hurt in her voice.

'You said I was the only man you have ever made love with. But even if you'd had hundreds of other lovers it wouldn't matter. I believe this baby is mine.'

'I still don't give a damn.' She tried to step past him, but Nico moved closer so that she was trapped by the counter behind her and him in front of her.

'I had more tests at a fertility clinic, and today I learned that my sperm count is normal and I am not infertile. The test I did years ago gave an inaccurate result.'

She shook her head. 'So on the strength of one unreliable test result and a lie your brother told you, you were judge and jury and found me guilty of a crime I didn't even know I was supposed to have committed.' Sienna ran her hand over her eyes, but when Nico touched her arm—wanting, needing to make a connection with her—she shrugged him off. 'You told me to get out of your life and I have done what you asked. I don't know why you have come here. I don't want to know. At the risk of repeating myself, *I don't care.*'

Nico was fascinated by the temper that made her eyes flash as fiery bright as the lightning that had lit the dark sky during the electrical storm on the night of Danny's wedding. The night their child had been conceived, he now knew. He also knew that there was only one course of action open to him, to them.

He stepped closer to her and captured her chin between his fingers, tilting her face up to his. 'I've come to marry you, of course.'

CHAPTER NINE

SIENNA LAUGHED AND LAUGHED. Even when Nico did not join in she laughed, because surely his statement had been a joke—a crass and tasteless joke, but a joke nevertheless.

'I'm glad you are not averse to the idea,' he drawled when she wiped away her tears of amusement—it was definitely amusement she felt. They were not tears of heartbreak, she assured herself.

'Not averse?' She jerked her chin out of his lean fingers. 'Nico, there is no way I will marry you. Never again. Not in this lifetime.'

He smiled, and God forgive her but she could not prevent herself from staring at his mouth that could be sensual or cruel but right at this moment was pure temptation. 'Why not?' he said mildly.

'Seriously, you need to ask? Why would I be idiotic enough to repeat the mistake we made ten years ago? Why would you? I'm not eighteen and scared of my father's temper, and you are not under pressure from your grandfather to do your duty and legitimise your child. You told me that you never wanted to set eyes on me again and I share that sentiment.'

Her tenuous control on her emotions shattered and she clenched her hands by her sides to stop herself from lashing out at him. 'Go away, Nico. Go to hell for all I care. Just keep away from me and my baby.'

'He is my son too, *cara*.'

'Don't.' She hated the way her insides melted and reminded herself that she hated *him*. But that huskily spoken *cara* had tugged on her traitorous heart.

'I know I screwed up in Italy, but I need to make my position clear. Maybe you hate me right now,' he murmured with an arrogance that made her grind her teeth. Nico would find it impossible to believe that any woman could hate him. The fact that she didn't hate him made Sienna furious with herself. He had treated her appallingly and she would not be taken in by his easy charm ever again. It had been the problem in the past. She had made it too easy for him. He hadn't had to try to win her. She'd rolled over like an eager puppy, she thought grimly.

But the indisputable fact was that she was expecting Nico's baby. 'If you think I'll agree to a DNA test while I'm pregnant, you can take a running jump,' she said sharply. 'A prenatal paternity test is an invasive procedure, and I refuse to do anything that could put the baby at risk. And anyway, there can only be one outcome. You are the father and if you are serious about wanting to have a role in your son's life I won't object. But this isn't the Dark Ages and it's ridiculous to suggest that we have to get married, especially when we tried it once before and it was a disaster.'

'So what is your suggestion?' Nico demanded.

The hard gleam in his eyes warned Sienna that he was angry. That made two of them, she thought. But her shock at seeing him again when she'd truly believed that she never would was having an effect on her. The fight drained out of her, and it didn't help that she was exhausted after a long day at work. She had been awake for a couple of hours before her alarm had gone off at six that morning, worrying about how she was going to manage to run her business and look after a baby. Especially with the Tutjo coup threatening her Marula oil supplier—she hoped the women and families at the cooperative were okay. It was also, she realised when she glanced at her watch, well past dinner time. She had an appetite like a horse at the moment and her stomach was reminding her that it was empty.

'I'm going home.' She pushed past him and headed towards the door. 'I suggest you go back to Italy. I'll contact you after the baby is born and you can decide then how involved you want to be.'

His rigid jaw warned her that he did not appreciate being spoken to like that. Nico always wanted to be in control. After a moment he said tersely, 'I'll take you home. My car is outside.'

'I prefer to walk. My flat's not far away.' But when she preceded him outside and locked the workshop, it was raining hard. Autumn had brought an end to the summer heatwave and the nights were drawing in. Nico's chauffeur opened the car door and Sienna decided there was no point getting soaked for the sake of her pride. 'If you go along the high street for about a mile, I live in a flat above the kebab shop,' she explained.

Nico slid into the car beside her and gave her a simmering look. 'The future Viscount Mandeville will not spend his formative years living above a kebab shop,' he said brusquely. He leaned forwards and murmured something to the driver, and seconds later the privacy screen slid up. Sienna shifted along the seat away from him but the evocative scent of his aftershave stirred memories of being in his arms, her face pressed against his neck while he used his hands and mouth to bring her body to the pinnacle of pleasure over and over again. She hated that she was so aware of him, hated her weakness and the stupid little flicker of hope inside her that maybe he didn't despise her now he knew she hadn't lied.

The smooth motion of the car made her feel sleepy, but when they stopped at a red light she peered out of the window at the neon-lit streets. There were no traffic lights on the route to her flat. 'This isn't the way to where I live.'

'I've arranged for us to have dinner at my hotel,'

Nico said coolly. 'I would like to have a proper, adult conversation with you about the future when we become parents to our child, who is the innocent one in all of this,' he added before she could argue.

Damn him for being right, Sienna thought heavily. Of course she wanted to do the best for her baby, and that meant she must put aside her resentment of Nico and at least try to establish a cordial relationship with him. 'I'm not dressed for dinner at a five-star hotel,' she muttered when the car stopped outside the hotel's grand entrance.

'You look fine.' Nico captured her hand in his, as if he expected her to run away. The glint in his blue eyes when he stared down at her made her heart pound. 'You look beautiful, always, Sienna,' he murmured.

Don't fall under his spell, she told herself as he escorted her into the hotel. If she hadn't been so famished she would have put up more resistance, but she felt light-headed—a sure sign that her blood sugars had dropped too low. 'Aren't we eating here?' she asked when Nico whisked her across the foyer and they passed the entrance to the hotel's restaurant.

'We'll have dinner in my suite so that we can be assured of privacy while we talk,' he said, ushering her into the lift.

'As long as talking is all you want to do?' She flushed when his brows rose, and instantly regretted her provocative comment that was a defence against the way he made her feel. She was fiercely aware of him but she did not know if he was still attracted to her. Although she was nearly four months pregnant her baby bump was barely showing. But she was conscious of other changes to her figure: her thickening waistline and fuller breasts. It didn't help that Nico was so incredibly handsome, she thought ruefully. The woman at the reception desk had practically drooled over him.

'I'm not planning to leap on you the minute we're alone,' he told her curtly, which should have reassured her but had the opposite effect.

The penthouse suite was ultra-modern—all moody colours on the walls and a lot of black glass and silver chrome. A table was set for two, and a butler served them dinner. Sienna remembered when Nico had come to her hotel room in York and they had made love throughout the night. They had been so hungry for each other. It seemed a lifetime ago when she had decided to enjoy a sex-without-strings affair with him. Now they were inextricably linked by the baby who was the result of their passion.

Her tension went up a notch when the butler left them alone, but Nico seemed in no hurry to talk, allowing her time to focus on the delicious food. The *boeuf en croute* melted in her mouth and she gave a sigh of contentment when she'd finished her dinner.

He sipped his wine and topped up her glass of sparkling water. 'Are you keeping well?'

She nodded. 'I had a scan last week, which is when I found out that I'm expecting a boy. Apparently everything is fine and I'm having a textbook pregnancy so far.' She bit her lip, aware of how quickly the situation could change. The miscarriage years ago had happened without warning. She had been excited that she was over halfway through her pregnancy but a few hours later she had held her lifeless baby in her arms.

'I'm looking after myself and eating well,' she told Nico. 'I was lucky that I didn't really suffer from morning sickness. Although if I'd felt worse, perhaps I would have realised earlier that I was pregnant.' She fell silent, remembering his reaction to the news of her pregnancy. He had been so horrible and said such hurtful things that she doubted she would ever forget them, even if she managed to forgive him.

She pulled her mind back to the present and looked at him, wishing she could read the thoughts behind his inscrutable expression. The distance between them was far wider than the table where they were sitting opposite one another. She didn't know how to breach it, or if she even wanted to.

'I can only spend a few days in England and I want you to come back to Lake Garda with me,' he said abruptly. 'I will arrange for a top obstetrician in Italy to oversee your care for the rest of your pregnancy.' Nico's jaw tightened when she shook her head. 'I want to be able to support you while you are pregnant and after the baby is born, but it will be difficult if I am in Italy and you are here. It makes sense for us to get married as soon as possible.'

'How can there be any sense in a marriage that neither of us wants?' Sienna said, frustrated.

His face hardened, determination stamped on his patrician features. 'My son will be born legitimate.'

'You can't force me to marry you.'

'Have you forgotten that I paid the rebels in Tutjo one million dollars for you?'

She made a choked sound, a mixture of anger at his arrogance and a sense of helplessness at the realisation that Nico would fight dirty if he had to. Beneath his civilised veneer he came from a bloodline of barons and warrior knights that stretched back through centuries of some of Europe's most violent history. 'I'll repay the money somehow,' she said stiffly, 'even if I have to work twenty hours a day.'

'You won't be able to work at all when the baby is born. Or are you planning to leave him in an all-day nursery when he's a week old while you pursue your career?'

'*You* have a career. Why shouldn't I?' she shot back at him. 'My skincare company might not be a multimillion-pound business like De Conti Leisure, but I started Fresh Faced with a small bank loan and now it turns over a healthy annual profit.'

'The point I am making is that you would not need to work if you were my wife.'

She gave an exasperated sigh. 'You are missing the point. I want to work and be financially independent. My mother stayed with my father even though he was a drunkard and a bully because she was financially reliant on him. She didn't have a good education or means to a career. I was determined that I wouldn't be caught in the same trap, which is why I studied for a degree and started my own business.'

Nico frowned. 'I wasn't suggesting that you would have to give up running Fresh Faced. If you marry me, we can employ a nanny to help with the baby so that you can continue to work.'

Sienna's head ached and she massaged her brow with her fingertips. The truth was that she did not know how she was going to manage to juggle work and motherhood. She was haunted by memories of losing her first baby, and in this pregnancy she was scared to hope that she would end up with a healthy baby in a few months' time.

'Would you have asked me to marry you if I was expecting a girl?'

Nico's gaze did not waver from hers. 'Of course.'

'I wondered if you wanted the baby because it's a boy.'

'The sex of our child makes no difference to me.' He hesitated. 'But the fact that you are having a boy *is* relevant. At the beginning of the last century the fifth Viscount Mandeville made a covenant which stipulates that only a *legitimate* firstborn

male can inherit the title and the Sethbury estate.
The baby you are carrying can only be my heir if
we are married. Would you deny our son his birthright, Sienna?'

'There isn't a baby yet.' She stared down at the
tablecloth while she struggled to hold back her tears.
She didn't know how she could bear it if she lost this
baby too. A part of her was tempted to let Nico take
over. If she agreed to marry him he would sweep her
into his wealthy, privileged lifestyle and she wouldn't
have to worry about paying the rent for her one-
bedroom flat that was not an ideal place to bring up
a child. For Nico it would be a marriage of convenience for the child's sake, which was the reason he
had married her ten years ago. But now, as then, it
wasn't enough for Sienna.

She picked up the cup of jasmine tea that Nico had
poured her instead of coffee at the end of the meal
and carried her drink over to the low table in front of
the sofa. With a sigh, she sat down and leaned back
against the cushions. Tiredness swept over her in a
great wave and her eyelids drooped. In a minute, she
would ask him to take her home, she told herself.

Sienna surfaced from a deep sleep. Last night she
had been exhausted and she'd slept better than she'd
done for weeks, she realised, giving a lazy stretch.
She didn't even remember arriving back at her flat
or putting her pyjamas on. Her hand met something

warm and solid that felt remarkably like a muscular, male body. She turned her head on the pillow and her heart clattered against her ribs when she stared into a pair of brilliant blue eyes. 'What are you doing in my bed…?' Her voice trailed away as she glanced around the room and discovered that she was in Nico's hotel room. In his bed.

'Buongiorno, cara,' he drawled.

She sat up and flushed when she discovered that she was wearing her bra and knickers. The bra was at least two sizes too small and her breasts spilled above the lacy cups. Quickly pulling the sheet up to cover her body, she said tautly, 'Did you undress me?'

'You fell asleep on the sofa after dinner and I didn't have the heart to wake you.'

'Oh, yes, you are all heart,' she snapped sarcastically, her cheeks burning hotter at the idea of him taking her clothes off. 'You should have woken me.' She stiffened when she tried to move her leg and discovered that it was trapped beneath Nico's hair-roughened thigh. Another shocking thought, worse than finding herself in bed with him, came into her mind. 'Did we…?'

The amusement disappeared from his eyes and he swore. 'No, we didn't make love. Is that the opinion you have of me, that I would have sex with you without your knowledge or consent?'

Sienna told herself that she must have imagined he sounded hurt. He flung back the sheet and stood up, and she did not know whether to feel relieved or disappointed when she saw that he was wearing a pair of black silk boxer shorts. 'No, I don't think you would do that,' she mumbled.

He let out his breath slowly but the tension between them was still tangible as anger and mistrust was replaced by a simmering awareness. 'I resisted you when you cuddled up to me so sweetly during the night, and I even managed to resist the temptation to satisfy my desire when you stroked your hands over every part of my body, and I do mean *every* part,' he said mockingly.

'I did not.' Sienna gave a silent groan as she recalled her very erotic dream in which she had tormented Nico with her hands and mouth. In her dream she had circled her fingers around his hard shaft— but perhaps she hadn't dreamed it!

She was too embarrassed to look at him when he sat down on the edge of the mattress. He slid his hand beneath her chin, tipping her face up so that she couldn't evade his gaze. A feral hunger sharpened his features and his eyes glittered when her tongue darted out to moisten her lips.

'Your subconscious knows what you want, even if you refuse to admit that you want me,' he said. 'There has always been this fire between us.'

'It's called lust,' she whispered.

'It doesn't matter what we label it. Whatever you think of me, the passion we have for each other is unique. I've never found anything to equal it, and neither have you or you would have had other lovers.'

'I dated a few other men.' She didn't want him to think she'd lived like a nun since their divorce, although it wasn't far from the truth, Sienna acknowledged.

'But you did not give your body to any of them because you are mine,' Nico growled. The possessiveness in his voice sent a tremor through her and she watched helplessly as his head descended. Where was her outraged denial? Where was her pride? taunted a voice inside her. Was she really going to lie there and let him kiss her?

And then he was doing just that and she made no attempt to stop him. His warm breath whispered over her lips and she expected him to claim her mouth with the same fierce possession that had been in his voice. But his kiss was as soft as gossamer. Gentle, almost reverent, healing the hurt that his damning accusations had wrought as he coaxed her lips apart.

She couldn't resist him, and in truth she did not want to. His skin felt like satin beneath her fingers when she put her hand on his shoulder and moved it up to his nape. She stroked his hair and then continued her exploration, discovering the sharp angles of his face and the rough stubble on his jaw. Her head fell back against the pillows and she opened her mouth beneath his as he deepened the kiss, sliding his lips over hers and tasting her with little sips that made her long for him to drink deep. But he was in control and when at last he lifted his mouth from hers she stared at him, unable to speak or think or move away from him, even though she knew she should do all three.

Warily she waited for him to mock her eager response to him. He knew now that she was hopelessly weak. As if he needed more power over her, she thought wryly.

'You mentioned an idea of establishing a new workshop for Fresh Faced, possibly in Paris,' he said. 'Have you found a suitable premises?'

Sienna remembered that she'd postponed a trip to Paris and gone to Italy with Nico for a party at Villa Lionard—a lifetime ago, it seemed. 'No, I've been busy with other things,' she said drily. 'The long-term plan is for me to set up another workshop in central Europe, and my assistant Carley will run the London workshop. But expanding the business will have to wait until after the baby is born.'

'Why not open a workshop in northern Italy? My office is in Verona and I want to bring our son up at Lake Garda. You can speak Italian and it would be the perfect solution.'

It was something to consider, Sienna conceded. She watched Nico put on his trousers before he crossed the room and took a shirt out of the wardrobe. Glancing around, she spied her clothes on a chair. When he disappeared into the en-suite bathroom, she jumped out of bed, intending to be dressed by the time he returned. She was halfway across the room when he walked back into the bedroom, and heat spread across her face when he stopped in his tracks.

'Don't stare at me,' she muttered self-consciously. 'My hips and bust are in competition to see which can expand faster.'

'You look gorgeous.' He came towards her, the undisguised hunger in his gaze causing molten warmth to pool between her thighs. 'Italian men appreciate a voluptuous female figure.' He grinned when her eyes flashed angrily. 'I am Italian, *cara*, and I love your curves. But you need a new bra.' He touched the red mark on her skin where the strap of her bra had cut in. 'Or better still, no bra,' he murmured, releasing the clasp before she realised his intention.

Freed from the restrictive garment, she took a deep breath and held it when Nico lightly circled one taut nipple with his finger. It felt so good. She wished he would tumble her down on the bed and kiss her breasts. Pregnancy had made her nipples ultra-sensitive.

But her pregnancy was the only reason he had come to look for her in London. The thought dropped into her brain, a cold, hard reality that Sienna could not ignore. Nico wanted his child and it was in his interest to keep her happy with sex. Furious with herself for allowing him to control her, she moved away from him and pulled on her jumper and trousers before zipping up her boots.

'I have somewhere in mind that could be an ideal premises for your new workshop,' Nico told her. 'I'll give you the rest of the week to hand over to your assistant who you said will manage Fresh Faced in London when you come to live at Villa Lionard.'

'I haven't agreed to live at the villa. I said I'll think about opening a workshop in Italy.' She bit her lip when she saw the determination on his face. 'Don't push it, Nico. After the way you treated me, you should be thankful that I am willing to consider the idea of sharing parenthood with you.'

'Would you put your pride before the best interests of our child?' he demanded. 'I can provide our son with two beautiful homes in England and Italy. If necessary, a court will have the final say on where he will grow up, and the decision will be made based on which of us can give our child the most stable and secure upbringing.'

Sienna opened her mouth but no words emerged. She felt sick as fear, shock and searing anger churned inside her. 'Are you saying that you will seek custody of the baby?'

'I hope it does not come to that,' Nico said coolly. 'But yes, I will do everything in my power to be a full-time father to my son and bring him up in Italy.'

'You really are a bastard,' she choked. She raced

over to the door, desperate to get away from him before he saw the tears that blurred her vision. But before she could step into the corridor he caught hold of her arm and spun her round to face him.

'Think what you like of me. But no one will be able to call my son a bastard,' he said harshly. 'You *will* marry me, Sienna. I advise you not to keep me waiting too long.'

CHAPTER TEN

THE FLOWERS ARRIVED later that afternoon. Two dozen red roses, each a perfect bloom with velvety petals and a sensuous fragrance that permeated through the workshop, even though Sienna left the flowers in a vase on the reception desk out of her sight.

The card attached to the bouquet simply had Nico's name scrawled across it. She did not know if the roses were a peace offering or a calculated ploy to try to win her round. An angry silence had simmered between them in the car when his chauffeur had driven them from the hotel to her flat, en route to taking Nico to the airport. Nico had looked at the shop front on Camden High Street with the name Ali's Kebabs over the door and muttered something uncomplimentary beneath his breath.

The next day a bouquet of lilies was delivered to the workshop and the day after that it was freesias, gerberas and daisies tied with a pink ribbon.

'Well, I think it's romantic that Nico is so keen to be reconciled with you,' Carley said at the end of the week, when Sienna plonked the latest delivery of exquisitely scented white orchids into a bucket of water. They had run out of vases.

'He's only keen to have his own way,' Sienna muttered. 'Nico doesn't like to take no for an answer.'

'How well you know me, *cara*.' A familiar, oh, so sexy voice came from the doorway. She spun round and stared at Nico as he strolled into the workshop. He was wearing faded jeans and a grey sweater topped by a tan leather jacket that looked buttersoft. Raindrops clung to his dark hair and he lifted a hand to push it off his brow. Sienna was aware that Carley's jaw had dropped. It wasn't fair that Nico was so gorgeous, she thought when she introduced him to her assistant and best friend.

'You had better come into my office,' she told him, furious with herself for the rush of hot jealousy she felt when he smiled at Carley. 'Are you in London on business or…um…pleasure?' She flushed when his eyes gleamed wickedly.

'It is always a pleasure to see you, Sienna,' he murmured. 'I have found premises for your new workshop and thought you would like to take a look at it.'

She frowned. 'In Italy, do you mean? When will I need to fly out?' During the last week she had come to the conclusion that establishing a branch of Fresh Faced in Italy made sense for the business and for her personally because it would allow her to combine work and motherhood. She was afraid that Nico had not made an idle threat when he'd said he would be prepared to fight for custody of their child. But if she found a place to live for her and the baby near to Villa Lionard, perhaps he would be content to visit whenever he wanted.

'The pilot is preparing my plane for the return flight to Verona, and my car is outside now to take us to the airport,' he said smoothly.

She bit her lip, angry that once again he thought he could simply take over her life. But it was Friday lunchtime, all the orders were up to date and for once she had the weekend free. There was no harm in going with him to see if the premises he had found could be turned into a workshop.

'I suppose Carley can take over here for the rest of the day,' she said reluctantly. 'But I'll have to go back to my flat and pack an overnight bag.'

'There's no need for you to bring anything. I've arranged for you to meet a personal shopper in Verona. It won't be long before you will need to wear maternity clothes,' he pointed out before she could argue.

Lake Garda in the autumn was astonishingly beautiful. The trees were a riot of red, gold and bronze, and the calm lake reflected the pink clouds in the sky above, stained by the sun as it slowly sank below the horizon.

Nico drove them from the airport in his scarlet

Ferrari. When he turned the car onto the driveway of Villa Lionard, the knot of tension in Sienna's stomach tightened as she remembered how he had dismissed her from the house and his life a month ago. Now he believed the baby she was expecting was his but she wasn't foolish enough to think he had sent her flowers as a romantic gesture. He wanted his son and she was a necessary part of the equation— at least she was until she gave birth, and only then if the baby survived.

'When are you taking me to see the new workshop?' she asked as she climbed out of the car. 'Is it in Verona?'

'It's here, and you can see it now.' He smiled at her look of surprise and wrapped his hand around hers. Instead of ushering her inside the villa, he led her around to the courtyard at the rear of the house and over to what had, a century or so ago, been a farm outhouse. The building had been turned into garages where Nico kept his collection of sports cars. But when he opened the door there were no cars inside.

'Welcome to your new workshop,' he said. 'What do you think of it?'

'It's impressive,' Sienna said slowly. She walked around the big space, noting the long work counter in the centre of the room and more worktops next to the double sinks along one wall. There were plenty of cupboards and shelves, as well as two fridges for storing the perishable ingredients she used in her products. At the far end of the workshop double-height windows looked out over Lake Garda, and, although the light was fading as dusk fell, she could see big containers on the patio where she could grow herbs and plants such as lavender and chamomile for her products. The workshop was perfect, she acknowledged, but she couldn't help feeling that she was being manipulated by Nico.

'Builders have worked all week to reconfigure the garages into a workspace for you,' he said.

'Where will you keep all your cars?'

'I intend to sell most of them. Becoming a parent will require me to give up some of the things I enjoy, but it will be a small price to pay when I have my son.'

Sienna wondered what other things he planned to give up. Sex-without-strings affairs with beautiful women, perhaps? Or would he just be more discreet when he took lovers?

'You don't seem very thrilled. If there is anything else you need, tell me.' He walked towards her, his eyes narrowing on her tense face. 'I had the workshop created so that you can live at the villa and continue to run your business after the baby is born. You told me that you want to carry on working.'

'I do,' Sienna muttered.

'So what's the problem?' he demanded, sounding annoyed by her lack of enthusiasm. He made her feel like a stroppy child, she thought angrily.

'You're the problem, Nico.' She made a frustrated sound when his brows lifted. 'The workshop is wonderful, and I'm grateful.' She almost choked on the word. She didn't feel grateful, she felt infuriated by his determination to control every situation, to control her. 'But you didn't create the workshop as a nice gesture to make me happy. You did it so that I wouldn't be able to refuse to move to Villa Lionard.'

His brows drew together in a heavy scowl. 'Why don't you want to move here? We agreed that it is the best place for the baby to live.'

'*I* didn't agree to anything. *You* threatened to take my baby away.'

He swore. 'I am trying to find a solution that will allow us to both be parents to our child.'

'You always want your own way.' Her voice rose as she gave vent to her temper that had simmered since Nico had swept back into her life and clearly expected her to be grateful that he wanted his baby. 'You think that if you send me flowers and present me with a workshop I will fall in with your plans just as I did when I was your teenage bride. But I am not the girl who worshipped the ground you walked on.'

Sienna broke off to snatch a breath. Nico looked stunned that she had the temerity to tell him a few home truths, but she didn't care. It was time he realised that he couldn't push her around. 'When I married you I was so in love with you and I would have done anything to make you happy. But you didn't love me and you didn't trust me.'

'How could I have known that Danny lied to me?' Nico said curtly.

'You could have asked me for the truth. You *should* have asked me.'

'He is my brother...'

'I was your *wife*.' She felt angrier than she had ever been in her life, and Nico's shuttered expression made her angrier still. She never knew what he was thinking. He never let her in. 'You haven't even apologised for the terrible things you accused me of when we found out about this pregnancy.' She hated that she couldn't hide the hurt in her voice, the faint quiver that betrayed her.

'I regret that I said those things,' he said gruffly. 'I regret that I allowed my brother's jealousy ten years ago to come between us, twice.' His gaze burned into hers and she sensed that he was struggling to maintain his iron self-control.

'There is no us, Nico.' It was painful to say and it made her realise how much she had secretly hoped there could be when they had met again eight years after their divorce. 'There never was *us*. There was sexual attraction that would have burned out if I hadn't fallen pregnant. I would have suffered a broken heart for a few months and you would have married someone more suitable to be your viscountess than the village publican's daughter.'

'But it didn't burn out,' he said, his eyes blazing as he walked towards her. 'Ten years after we first made love on a windswept moor, the chemistry between us is as combustible as it ever was.'

Sienna shook her head but he kept coming closer, backing her up against the work counter and stretching his arms out on either side of her so that she was caged in. Too late, she realised that she had unleashed the tiger, but she did not turn away when he lowered his head so that his warm breath grazed across her lips. Her heart clattered against her ribs when he tangled his fingers in her hair. Desire ran like quicksilver in her blood. 'Do you want me to do this?'

All she could do was whisper, 'Yes,' then he crushed her lips beneath his.

Relief swept through Nico when Sienna opened her mouth to the demands of his and responded to his kiss. The force of her anger had been like a wild storm. He'd thought he had lost her, and he was shocked by how much it bothered him. If she walked away from him, he knew it was what he deserved. He had let her down badly and she did not trust him, but somehow he would convince her that if she married him he would never give her a reason to doubt his commitment to their marriage or their child.

He fisted her hair and deepened the kiss, tangling his tongue with hers in an erotic dance that set his blood on fire. She wrenched her mouth free, her eyes glinting like silver flames. 'Sex doesn't solve anything,' she told him bitterly.

'Let's see, shall we?' He sought her lips again, but she evaded his mouth and sank her teeth into the side of his neck. 'Wildcat,' he growled, supremely turned on by her fierceness. 'So you want to play rough, do you? I hope you can take as good as you give.' He kissed his way up her throat before he bit her earlobe. She gasped and he smothered the sound with his mouth, kissing her with mounting hunger as she threaded her fingers into his hair and gave a hard tug.

'I hate what you do to me, the way you make me feel,' she muttered, anger and vulnerability darkening her eyes when they came up for air. 'I hate myself for responding to you like a sex addict when I don't even like you.'

'It's the same for me,' he told her, catching her hand and holding it over the burgeoning proof that he was very, very aroused. 'I only have to look at you and I'm desperate. But as well as desiring you, I like you, Sienna.' It was a truth he could not deny to himself or to her. 'I admire your independent spirit, your determination and your compassion, and I hope our son will grow up to have those qualities.'

Tears shimmered in her eyes. 'You say these things but I don't know if I can believe you.' Her voice cracked. 'I don't know how to handle you.'

He circled his hips against her hand where it was

resting on his crotch and groaned when she explored the hard ridge of his erection through his trousers. 'You are handling me perfectly, *cara*.'

Her dress was a wrap-around style and he untied the belt and ran his hands greedily over her body when the dress fell open. Quickly dispensing with her bra, he cradled her heavy breasts in his hands.

'Your breasts are bigger.' He did not try to hide his satisfaction. Pregnancy had made her body softer and even more sensual. Nico was impatient to discover every inch of her new voluptuous shape, to taste her vanilla-scented skin. He bent his head and drew one taut nipple into his mouth, enjoying the husky moans she made as he sucked hard before transferring his mouth to her other nipple and feasting on the cherry-red peak.

She gave a startled gasp when he lifted her and sat her on the edge of the work counter. Her eyes were wide, the pupils dilated as he tugged her dress off. 'If I'd known you were wearing stockings I would have had my hands on you long before now,' he said rawly, running his fingers over the lacy bands at the top of her thighs. Her legs looked gorgeous in sheer black stockings and the sweet scent of her arousal surrounded him when he pushed the panel of her panties to one side and buried his face between her thighs.

'Nico.' Her moans grew louder as he ran the tip of his tongue over her opening and then pushed it into her moist heat. She tasted of cream and the heavenly musk of her femininity heightened his desire as he pushed her legs wider apart and teased the tight nub of her clitoris with his tongue.

She arched backwards, thrusting her hips towards him while she supported herself with her hands flat on the counter. 'Oh, God, Nico, I want you inside me.'

He wanted that too. He wanted her so badly that his hands shook as he opened his zip and freed his erection from his trousers. She was so beautiful. Nico felt drunk with desire as he studied her creamy skin and the flush of rose pink on her cheeks and breasts. Her burgundy hair gleamed like raw silk on her shoulders.

He pushed her down so that she was lying on her back on the counter and tugged her panties off before he climbed on top of her, shoving her legs apart with his thigh. 'You are so wet, *cara*,' he said hoarsely when he slid a finger inside her and then withdrew it and licked her sweetness from his skin.

She wrapped her legs around his back, her fingers attacking his shirt buttons before she ran her hands over his bare chest. 'Now,' she said fiercely. 'I want you *now*.'

Her boldness excited him, and knowing that he was the only man who had ever possessed her evoked an odd tightness in his chest. Eyes locked with hers, he pressed forwards so that the tip of his manhood pressed against her entrance, and then he slid in deep, every one of his muscles locked as he fought to control the raging fire that threatened to consume him.

'*Sei mio,*' he whispered, his mouth pressed to her throat. In a distant recess of his mind an alarm bell rang. Possessiveness was an unknown emotion to him. And yet when he thrust into her, faster, harder, and took them both to the edge before they fell into the abyss together, a voice inside him insisted, *Mine.*

A long time later, when his heart-rate had returned to something like normal, Nico lifted himself off her and refastened his trousers. He looked at Sienna and found her watching him from beneath the sweep of her lashes.

'I will never be able to make my skincare creams here without remembering that we used this work counter for a very different reason,' she said ruefully.

'But you will set up a branch of Fresh Faced at Villa Lionard.' He made it a statement rather than a question and she gave him a measured look but did not disagree. He lifted her down from the counter and helped her into her clothes before he took hold of her hand and led her outside and across the courtyard to the main house. 'You can move into the villa immediately. I'll show you to your room.'

At the top of the stairs he turned down a corridor and opened the door of the master suite. Sienna followed him into the room, and Nico found that he disliked the wary expression in her eyes. 'This is your room,' she said guardedly.

'*Our* room, from now on.' He drew her into his arms and kissed away her frown. 'You said that sex doesn't solve anything, but I disagree. Our physical compatibility has never been in doubt.'

'The fact that we are good together in bed is hardly a stable base on which to build the kind of trusting relationship we will need when we become parents.'

'Are you suggesting that love is stable? A flimsy and in many cases transient emotional response is far more likely to fail. And when it does, the fallout can be much more damaging to a child caught between two parents whose love has turned to hatred and bitter acrimony.'

Nico swung away from Sienna and strode across the room to stare out of the window. It was completely dark now and the lake was outlined by the twinkling lights of the houses and villages that hugged the shore. 'I love how peaceful it is here,' he said abruptly. 'But my mother was bored at the villa and rarely visited—which is probably why I found it so peaceful.' After a moment he said, 'I was twelve when my mother tried to take her own life the first time.'

He heard Sienna gasp and saw her reflection in the window pane when she sat down on the edge of the bed. 'I had no idea. You didn't say much about your childhood while we were married.'

Nico remembered she had said that they had been

strangers on their wedding day. 'It wasn't something I found easy to talk about.' His jaw clenched. 'I still don't. As a boy, knowing that I couldn't make my mother happy so that she would want to live was hard. I felt I had let her down even though the cause of her unhappiness was my father. I blamed myself for not being around to comfort her. I was away at boarding school for most of the time and, to be honest...' he grimaced '...it was a relief to go back to school or spend part of the holidays at Villa Lionard with my Italian grandparents, away from my parents' rows and my mother's tears.'

'Jacqueline wasn't your responsibility,' Sienna said gently. 'What actually happened?'

'Danny and I were staying at Sethbury Hall for the summer. My parents had separated by then, and my father had gone to live in Paris with his latest mistress.'

He raked a hand through his hair, not certain why he felt a need to open up to Sienna about events in his childhood that he'd never told anyone else. 'My mother had promised to take me and my brother out for the day, but when she hadn't got up by lunchtime, I went to her room and found her unconscious in bed. Her skin was grey and cold and I thought she was dead.' Twenty years later, Nico remembered as if it had happened yesterday the icy shock that had slithered down his spine when he'd touched his mother's limp hand. 'She had taken an overdose of sleeping pills and left a note in which she blamed my father's infidelity for her unhappiness.'

'I'm so sorry.' Sienna's voice sounded closer and when he turned his head he found she was standing beside him. 'It would have been a terrible experience for an adult, let alone a twelve-year-old boy.' She slipped her hand into his and squeezed his fingers, compassion darkening her eyes as she asked, 'Did Jacqueline make other suicide attempts?'

'One other, and she was very nearly successful.' Nico gripped Sienna's small hand that fitted so perfectly into his much larger one. 'My father was a serial adulterer but my mother was besotted with him.'

'I only met Franco a few times but I remember that he was very handsome. He reminded me of one of those matinee idols like Clark Gable or Cary Grant.'

'He had something—charisma, charm—that made women throw themselves at him.'

'Like father, like son,' Sienna said drily.

Nico shook his head. 'No, I am not like him in one crucial respect. I enjoy sex and I enjoy women but I always make it clear at the start of an affair that I won't fall in love. My father got an ego boost from making women fall in love with him. He played with their hearts before he trampled on them. In many ways my mother was just as bad. She said she loved Franco but what she really wanted was to own him.

Her possessiveness bordered on maniacal and she drove my father away with her jealousy.'

'My parents' marriage was no better than yours.' Sienna grimaced. 'The only difference is that mine didn't row, they rarely spoke to each other at all. Surely we have just given two very good examples of why we shouldn't get married.'

'On the contrary. Our parents' marriages failed because of the expectation that falling in love is a guarantee of happy ever after. But love is a fantasy, and the reality is that marriage between two people who share the same values and aspirations—in our case to be good parents to our child—stands a much better chance of lasting.'

'We lasted two years,' she reminded him.

'It went wrong between us before because emotions were involved.'

'Not your emotions, Nico.' Sienna's tone was as dry as a desert. 'Don't worry,' she said when he frowned. 'I grew out of my infatuation with you. But do you really believe that a marriage without emotions can succeed? Is a loveless marriage what you want?'

Nico could not comprehend why Sienna's question made his heart clench. Of course he wanted a partnership without the dramas and histrionics that had littered his parents' relationship, he assured himself.

'More important to me than anything else is that my son is born legitimate,' he admitted. 'After my father died, I learned that he had a number of illegitimate children. As far as I am aware Franco never had any contact with his offspring. I don't know their identities, or even how many other children he fathered. His lawyers dealt with the paternity claims and the women were paid off.'

He met Sienna's startled gaze. 'I will not abandon my child. And I know how much you want to be a mother. Our son deserves for us to be the best parents we can possibly be and although it might be considered old-fashioned to marry for the sake of our baby, I believe it is the right thing to do.' He looked down at their linked hands and lifted her fingers up to press his lips against her knuckles. 'What do you say, *cara*? Will you be my wife?'

CHAPTER ELEVEN

'I NEED SOME time to think about it.' Sienna ignored the leap her heart gave at Nico's proposal. He had made it clear that he was suggesting a marriage of convenience and it was crucial she did not involve her heart in her decision.

'What is there to think about?' he demanded, his blue eyes glittering with impatience. He pulled her into his arms and held her hard up against his whip-cord body. 'We can make it work, *cara*. We are both passionate people and you will never find another man who can satisfy you like I can.'

She stiffened, angered by his arrogance. But she was strong enough to match his self-assurance, and she would not allow him to dominate her because she knew that he was as much a slave to their mutual desire as she was. Her weakness for him was also her strength, Sienna realised, and the proof was in the low groan he gave when she pressed her pelvis against his rock-hard arousal.

'Witch,' he muttered against her mouth before he

claimed her lips in a fierce kiss that left her breathless and trembling when he finally lifted his head and stared into her eyes. 'Marry me and I swear you will not regret it.'

She fought the temptation to give into his strong will. 'Ask me again in a month. I'll be over twenty-two weeks then. Hopefully.' He looked puzzled and she said quietly, 'I miscarried at twenty-two weeks and I don't want to tempt fate.'

'You're superstitious?'

'I'm scared,' she admitted, looking away from him. 'I want this baby so much and I don't know how I will bear it if something goes wrong.' She expected Nico to casually dismiss her fears but he slid his hand beneath her chin and tilted her face up to his. The tenderness in his expression stole around her heart.

'The scan and other checks you had in England showed no problems,' he reminded her softly. 'Next week you have an appointment with one of the highest-regarded obstetricians in Italy who will care for you for the remainder of your pregnancy. And I intend to make sure that you eat well and get plenty of rest,' he said, lifting her into his arms and carrying her over to the bed. 'Starting now.'

Sienna lay back on the pillows and gave him a quizzical look when he stretched his tall frame out beside her on the bed. He was so gorgeous, and when he smiled at her the way he was doing now she was ready to believe that they could make marriage work a second time around. 'Do you need to rest too?' she murmured, trailing her fingers down his shirt and slipping them beneath the waistband of his trousers. 'Because I'm not tired.'

His eyes flashed with wicked intent as he flipped her dress up to her waist and stroked the bare strip of skin above the lacy band of her stocking top. 'In that case we had better find something else to occupy us before dinner, hadn't we, *mia bellezza*?'

A week went by, and then another. Sienna was so busy hiring staff and getting the new workshop up and running that she forgot her initial doubts about agreeing to move to Villa Lionard. As autumn slipped into winter, Nico seemed determined to build the foundations of a strong relationship with her. He took an interest in her business and advised her on marketing strategies to promote the Fresh Faced ethos of using sustainable and natural ingredients. Sienna had been relieved when the coup in Tutjo ended with the King returned to power, and the women's cooperatives were safe and able to harvest Marula oil once more.

The first heavy snowfall of the winter had draped the mountains in a white cloak that sparkled in the afternoon sunshine. From the workshop Sienna could see through the tall windows a couple of sailing boats skimming over the lake. The water was as blue as the cloudless sky and when she'd walked across to the workshop from the villa, the air was cold and crisp.

The sound of a car pulling up in the courtyard caused her heart to skip a beat. Nico had been away on a business trip for two days, and, although he had phoned her numerous times, she couldn't wait to see him again. She heard his footsteps on the cobbles and then his tall frame filled the doorway. He looked impossibly handsome in a grey wool coat. His black hair gleamed in the sunshine and his blue eyes were the colour of the sky.

'Nico.' Sienna flew across the workshop and into his open arms, tilting her face up as he bent his head and claimed her mouth in a deeply sensual kiss.

'Mmm, that was some welcome,' he murmured. 'I think you must have missed me while I was away, *cara.*'

The satisfaction she heard in his voice reminded her to curb her enthusiastic greeting. 'I've been so busy that I barely noticed you weren't here,' she said airily.

An odd expression flickered on his face, but then it was gone, and Sienna told herself she must have imagined that he'd looked hurt. She felt a fluttering movement inside her and caught hold of his hand, pressing it against the firm swell of her stomach. She had been living at the villa for over a month, and maybe it was superstitious but she'd felt so relieved when she'd safely passed twenty-two weeks in her pregnancy. An ultrasound scan a few days ago had shown that her baby son was a good size and had a strong heartbeat, and she'd dared to start planning the colour scheme for the nursery.

'There, did you feel him move?' she asked Nico. They shared a smile when, right on cue, the baby kicked.

'Come back to the house. I have something to show you.' He looped his arm around her shoulders as they walked across the courtyard. Sienna loved the companionship between them that had emerged gradually over the last weeks. Their relationship might have got off to a rocky start but they were both trying to move on from the past.

'I thought you were going to stay away for one more night,' she said when they were in the sitting room and Nico stoked the fire that was burning in the hearth.

'I raced through my business meetings today so that I could fly home to be with you.' His voice was very deep, his accent more pronounced than usual, and Sienna's heart leapt at the realisation that he had meant it. He took a small package out of his brief-case and handed it to her. She tore off the wrapping paper and gave a soft cry of delight as she studied the photograph of a 4D scan image of their baby that Nico had had framed.

'Thank you. The picture is so clear, isn't it? It's so sweet that the baby is sucking his thumb.'

'Close your eyes,' he told her, 'and open your mouth.'

'Are you going to tell me why?'

'You have to trust me, *cara*.'

As Sienna obediently closed her eyes it occurred to her that she did trust him implicitly. She opened her mouth and then gave a sigh of pleasure when she tasted chocolate on her tongue. Her lashes swept upwards and she watched Nico take another chocolate out of a box of the finest Swiss confectionery and pop it between her lips. 'I *love* chocolate,' she murmured.

'I know. And you love kittens, and orphaned orangutans,' he said drily.

She grinned. 'The head of the orangutan sanctuary in Borneo was very grateful for the donation you made after we watched a documentary on TV about how orangutans are losing their natural habitat.'

Sienna glanced over at the two kittens asleep on the rug in front of the fire. Nico had brought them back to the villa a couple of weeks ago after she'd told him that she had always wanted a cat, but couldn't keep one at her flat on a busy London street. Charlie and Tiggs were adorable bundles of mischief. It was becoming increasingly hard to imagine leaving Villa Lionard and Nico, she thought ruefully. The villa felt like her home, and as the days passed—not to mention the incredible nights when Nico made love to her with passion coupled with an inherent tenderness that wrapped around her heart—she knew that she was falling ever deeper in love with him.

'I have one more surprise for you, but you will have to wait until tomorrow. Don't pout or I will have to kiss you, and you know where that always leads,' he said, kissing her anyway.

'Are you sure I can't persuade you to divulge your secret?' she murmured, trailing her fingers over the bulge evident beneath his trousers.

Nico drew her down onto the sofa. 'My lips are sealed, but I have no objection to you trying, *cara mia*.'

'I know you offered to teach me to ski, but I didn't think you meant now, when I'm five months pregnant,' Sienna said the next day when they were in the car and Nico drove past a road sign pointing to Malcesine Monte Baldo.

He laughed. 'Don't worry, we won't be skiing. But we are going to the top of the mountain in a cable car.'

'For any particular reason?'

He turned his head and gave her a look that she couldn't decipher. It was ridiculous to think he seemed nervous, she told herself. 'You'll find out soon,' was all he would say.

They took the cable car from the base station in the picturesque little town of Malcesine. Even in winter the area was a magnet for tourists and Sienna was surprised that she and Nico had a cabin to themselves, until he explained that he had booked a private trip for them. 'The cabin rotates as the cable car ascends, giving a three-hundred-and-sixty-degree view of the lake and mountains,' he said. 'On a clear day like today it's quite something.'

'The view is breathtaking.' Sienna was blown away by the sheer scale of the huge blue lake beneath them and the mountains soaring towards the sky, their snow-covered peaks glistening in the bright sunshine. 'I've never seen anything so beautiful.'

'Neither have I,' Nico said softly. But he wasn't looking at the view. He was staring at her, and her breath caught in her throat when he reached into his coat pocket and withdrew a small velvet box. He opened it and took out an exquisite oval-shaped sapphire ring surrounded by glittering diamonds. 'Will you marry me, Sienna?'

Her heart collided with her ribs. He had not mentioned marriage since he'd asked her the day he had brought her to Villa Lionard more than a month ago. Then, she had been uncertain about accepting what was still in essence a marriage of convenience. But Sienna had decided that she could not deny her son his birthright. Although Nico had not spoken of love, they had formed a close bond, and she believed that he cared for her a little. Her heart yearned for more, but she had learned that you couldn't always have what you wanted. And perhaps in time he would grow to love her in the way that she loved him, wholeheartedly and unreservedly, she told herself.

'Yes.' Her hand trembled when he slid the ring onto her finger. It fitted perfectly, as if it belonged there, just as her heart belonged to Nico.

Swept up on a wave of optimism, she felt sure that it would only be a matter of time before he fell in love with her. But for now she must suppress the joy that exploded in her heart and quell the choir of angels singing inside her. Time and patience were on her side. His beautifully romantic proposal had revealed a softer side to him, and when they were married she would have a lifetime to try to breach his defences and reach his heart that he guarded so well.

She lifted her hand up and watched the diamonds catch fire in the bright sunlight. Smiling at Nico, she said calmly, 'I agree that in the circumstances marriage is the most sensible thing to do.'

Of course marriage was a sensible option; the only option he would accept, Nico brooded. Obviously he was glad Sienna understood that his proposal had been a practical solution. So why did the word *sensible* stick in his throat during lunch at a restaurant on the summit of the mountain? He had eaten here before and knew the food was good, but his appetite had disappeared.

'Have you any thoughts on when you would like the wedding to take place?' she asked when she finished her plate of *tagliatelle* and gave a sigh of satisfaction.

'In a month. We have to give notice of our intention to marry.'

She nodded. 'It makes sense to get the wedding out of the way well before the baby is due.'

'Indeed, *cara*,' he said through gritted teeth.

'Are you all right? You haven't eaten much of your lunch.' Sienna stared at him across the table. 'Are you having second thoughts about us getting married? It was your idea. It doesn't matter to me, and it won't matter to the baby if we are married or we live together as we have done for the past month.'

'It matters that our son is legitimate when he is born,' he growled, instantly regretting his curt tone when Sienna bit her lip. What the hell was the matter with him? Nico wondered. Why did he feel a strong desire to walk around the table and kiss her until she was flushed and breathless and desperate for him to make love to her? He had no idea why he wanted to shatter her calm composure but if she uttered the word *sensible* one more time he would not be responsible for his actions.

'We'll go to Sethbury Hall to tell Iris and Rose that you are pregnant and announce our engagement. I'm surprised you haven't told your grandmother about the baby. Why did you keep your pregnancy a secret?'

'I felt embarrassed.'

'Embarrassed. Why?' He was shocked by her

reply and wondered if she was ashamed to be expecting his child.

'It is the second time that I accidentally conceived your baby.' There was a defensive note in Sienna's voice. 'Rose was bound to ask me who the father is, but the situation between us was complicated, and it was easier to say nothing while my pregnancy wasn't showing. Unlike now.' She stood up and gave a rueful glance down at her swollen belly.

Throughout lunch, Nico had been unable to take his eyes off Sienna. He'd watched the sunlight bring out the myriad shades of red in her hair: burgundy, auburn and copper tones that complemented her peaches-and-cream complexion. Her smoky grey eyes were fringed by long lashes a shade darker than her hair. And as for her mouth… He swallowed hard. Her mouth was to die for. He knew how soft it felt beneath his when he kissed her, and memories of how she used her tongue with such devastating effect on his body sent a hot rush of desire down to his groin.

He pulled his mind to the present. 'You look beautiful,' he told her gruffly. 'I love seeing the evidence that my child is inside you and growing bigger and stronger every day.'

They walked out of the restaurant and she turned her head and gave him a speculative look. '*Love*, Nico? I didn't know the word was in your vocabulary. Does it mean that you will love our son?'

'Of course I will.' He was taken aback by her

question. 'I am not devoid of feelings.' He'd have no problem loving his baby, who would look to him for care and protection—and who would not leave him. The thought slid into Nico's consciousness. A baby wouldn't be able to take a handful of sleeping pills or walk away from him without a backward glance. He exhaled slowly, wishing he knew what Sienna was thinking behind her cool grey gaze.

'Good,' she said gravely. 'Our baby deserves to have our unconditional love.' Something moved in her eyes: a question that Nico could not answer. But perhaps he imagined he saw a flicker of hurt on her face when his silence stretched for too long. 'We had better get on with organising a wedding,' she said, stepping away from him. 'I think it will be sensible to keep it a low-key event, don't you?'

Rain streamed down the window panes of Sethbury Hall but in the drawing room the flames leaping in the hearth were reflected in the oak-panelled walls and lent the room a rosy glow.

'Your engagement ring is stunning,' Iris said as she inspected the sapphire and diamond cluster on Sienna's finger. 'I understand that the wedding will be in Verona. A simple register office ceremony with a couple of close friends as witnesses, Nico told me.'

'Yes, we decided that a low-key wedding would be best,' Sienna said, patting her stomach, which seemed to expand daily. 'I would look like a ship in full sail if I wore a traditional white wedding gown.'

'That's not true.' Nico was leaning against the mantelpiece. He looked over at her and gave her a sexy smile that heated her blood. 'You look gorgeous whatever you wear, and you are even more beautiful wearing nothing at all.'

'Nico!' Fiery colour stained Sienna's cheeks and she could not look at his grandmother or her Grandma Rose.

Iris laughed. 'Pregnancy is often a very passionate time for a couple,' she said cheerfully. 'You are looking well, Sienna. That jade-green of your dress is lovely with your colouring. Being pregnant suits you.' She turned to Sienna's grandmother. 'Don't you think so, Rose?'

'I think that being in love is what makes Sienna and Nico both look so content,' Rose said softly.

Sienna jerked her gaze from Nico and looked down at her hand, pretending to study her ring. She sensed the tension that gripped him. She wanted to say something to fill the awkward silence, but she could hardly blurt out the truth to their grandmothers that their marriage was a practical arrangement.

She was relieved when Iris changed the subject. 'Domenico, while I remember, will you come and look at some documents my lawyer wants me to sign? I left them in the study.'

'I'll read them now, before lunch,' Nico said

abruptly. Sienna looked up at the same time that he glanced over at her and she wondered why he was frowning. He'd been in a strange mood ever since they had arrived at Sethbury Hall. She suspected that he missed his brother, whom he had not spoken to since he'd learned of Danny's lies.

'It's time to forget what happened in the past,' she had told Nico. 'You need to forgive Danny.'

'How can you say that after what he did? My brother's lies drove us apart.'

'No. Our mistrust of each other was what drove us apart,' she'd said flatly. 'We can't blame other people for the mistakes we made in our first marriage.'

After Nico pushed his grandmother in her wheelchair out of the room, Grandma Rose reached over and patted Sienna's hand. 'I am so glad that you and Nico are marrying for love. I see it in the way you look at him. And his eyes are full of love for you.'

Sienna bit her lip. 'Nanna...' she whispered, but her grandmother did not hear her.

'It was very different when I married your grandfather,' Rose said. 'I was pregnant with your father, and in those days being an unmarried mother was not accepted like it is now. My parents expected Peter to marry me, and he did his duty and proposed to me.' She sighed. 'I was madly in love with him. I knew he didn't share my feelings but I hoped he would fall in love with me once we were married.'

'Did he?' Sienna's grandfather had died when she

was a child and she had vague memories of a dour, short-tempered man.

'No. He resented the marriage and felt trapped. For a long time—too long—I thought things would change and we would grow closer, but Peter started to drink heavily and my feelings for him faded.'

'Why did you stay in a marriage that made you both unhappy?'

'We both loved our son—your father—and we stayed together for his sake. But our sour relationship affected Clive. When he grew up he spoke to me disrespectfully just as his father did, and when he married your mother I'm sorry to say that he treated her badly and drank heavily like his father.'

Rose wiped away a tear. 'I spent much of my life waiting for love that never happened. I thought I was doing the right thing for my son by staying in a loveless marriage, but the truth is that your father would have had a happier childhood if Peter and I had separated.'

The conversation moved on to other things, but Sienna could not concentrate as a dawning terrible realisation turned her blood to ice in her veins. There were glaring similarities between her grandmother's relationship with her husband, and her own relationship with Nico. Like Sienna, Grandma Rose had been in love, but her husband had only married her out of duty because she had been pregnant. Sienna's father had been damaged by growing up with parents trapped in an unhappy marriage, and it had affected Clive's relationship with Rose and with Sienna's mother.

She looked over at her grandmother and saw that she had nodded off to sleep. Iris returned to the drawing room and said that Nico had gone for a workout in the gym before lunch. Sienna's heart was thumping when she walked out of the house and along the path to the old stable block, which had been converted into a gym. She had to talk to Nico and find out if she had been deluding herself to hope that the attention he'd paid her while they had lived together at Villa Lionard meant he felt something for her.

She opened the door of the gym and stepped inside. Nico had his back to her and was pummelling a punchbag with his fists. He was stripped to the waist and a pair of sweatpants sat low on his hips. For several moments she simply stood there in the shadows and watched the ripple of his hard muscles and the gleam of his satiny skin beaded with sweat. He was so beautiful. That lean, hard body was a work of art, and the power in every blow he landed on the punchbag was an indication of his physical strength.

There was something untamed about him. Untameable, Sienna acknowledged. Nico would never be owned. Even more powerful than his muscular physique was his mental strength. There was not a hint of vulnerability about this man, and the truth hit her then that Nico viewed love as a weakness.

She made a muffled sound, trying to contain her emotions, but he must have heard her, and he spun round, a concerned expression on his face when he saw her. '*Cara*, what's wrong?' he demanded, pulling off his boxing gloves as he strode over to her. 'You are so pale. Are you unwell?' His voice sharpened. 'The baby…?'

She bit her lip. Of course he was concerned for the baby. The child they had created together in the heat of passion was the only reason he had put an engagement ring on her finger, and why he was so determined to put a wedding band beside it. 'I feel fine,' she assured him, the lie battering her bruised heart.

Nico's look of relief shattered her control over the storm of feelings swirling inside her. His relief was for the baby. Everything he felt was for the baby but he felt nothing for her, and it *hurt*.

'I can't do it, Nico,' she said, her voice cracking. 'I can't go through with a loveless marriage.'

He stiffened, and she sensed his barriers go up, shutting her out. 'We agreed—' he began, but she cut him off.

'I only agreed to marry you because I thought… I hoped that you would love me eventually. But I saw your face when Rose commented that we have the look of love. I saw rejection in your eyes when you glanced at me.' His expression had pierced her heart like an arrow.

Nico put his hands on her shoulders and ignored her attempts to pull free. 'Why are you so hung up on love?' he said harshly. 'What we had in Italy—friendship, trust, affection—why aren't those things enough?'

'Because I need more.' The pain in Sienna's chest was so intense that she could barely breathe. Her lungs felt constricted as the scales fell from her eyes and she saw the truth that she had been hiding from because it was so agonising. 'I want to love and be loved and I realised today that I can't accept anything less.'

'Love is a fool's game,' he gritted. 'I saw how loving my father almost destroyed my mother, and I promised myself that I would never make the mistakes my parents made.'

'But you haven't shut love out of your life completely. You said you will love your son. And I have seen the love you have for your grandmother and your brother.' Sienna twisted out of his grip and stared at his face, searching for some small sign of softening, but she saw none. He was granite down to his core.

'It's just me that you don't love,' she choked. 'If I refuse to marry you I will deny our son his birthright, but it is better that, than for him to grow up afraid of love like his father is.'

CHAPTER TWELVE

HE WAS NOT AFRAID. Nico slammed his fists into the punchbag. *Dio*, what was it with women and their need for a fairy tale that only existed in fiction? He had witnessed the dark side of love; the jealousy and power play, the empty bottle of pills on his mother's bedside table, the wail of an ambulance's siren.

Who wanted to live on an emotional roller coaster? He had been a boy when he'd decided to jump off that particular ride and stick to something safer…

Because he was afraid to fall in love.

The truth hit Nico harder than the blows he landed on the punchbag. He had locked his heart away and thrown away the key when his mother had tried to end her life that she'd decided was not worth living without the love of Nico's father, who had been a serial adulterer incapable of loving anyone other than himself. His mother hadn't appreciated the impact of her suicide attempts on her young sons.

Love *hurt*. It was why he had avoided that pernicious emotion, but despite his determination to live his life on his terms, Sienna had swept back into his life like a tornado and made him want the one thing he had told himself he had no need of. The one thing he could not control.

Damn her for forcing him to face the issue he was desperate to ignore, he thought savagely as he tore off his boxing gloves and strode out of the gym. He had been tempted to go straight after Sienna when she'd left five minutes ago, but he'd held back, not prepared to acknowledge that the sight of her tears had ripped his heart out.

Give her time to calm down, he'd told himself. Let the storm pass and when she was in a more reasonable frame of mind he would convince her that they were fine without the gut-wrenching, terrifying emotion that he knew love was.

He walked back to the house through the rain that had started to fall again from the leaden sky. After quickly checking the rooms on the ground floor and not finding Sienna there, he ran upstairs and along the corridor to the master suite. It was empty, but he immediately noticed her engagement ring on the coffee table.

Hell. Clenching his fists by his sides, he glanced across to the window and something outside caught his attention. A figure in a vivid green dress was hurrying along the path and through the gate that led from the garden of Sethbury Hall directly onto the moors.

Sienna was leaving him *again*!

Nico heard his blood thunder in his ears. Emotions he had kept at bay since he had run out of his mother's bedroom crying, 'Mama is dead,' surged through him like a tsunami, obliterating his self-control and leaving pain and fury in its wake. How could Sienna walk away from him? If she loved him she would stay with him. If his mother had loved him she would not have swallowed the pills.

He watched the green-clad figure become smaller as Sienna ran across the moors and disappeared in the mist. *'Don't leave me!'* he roared. The silence that answered him in the empty room was a mocking reminder that she had gone.

This was why he hated love. This burning sensation beneath his breastbone, this feeling as if he had swallowed shards of glass, this stinging sensation behind his eyelids. The woman he loved was walking away, but he wouldn't let her go. He *couldn't* let her go because losing her would destroy him.

Sienna stumbled through the bracken on her way to the ruins, blinded by her tears and the rain that stung her face and soaked her hair and clothes. She needed to get away. To run away from the agony of loving a man who would never love her. Loving hurt. Nico was right to treat love as if it were a terrible, infectious disease. Once you were exposed to it you were doomed. Better then to keep well away from it.

She heard the sound of her panting breaths and slowed her pace, afraid that her frantic escape from Sethbury Hall, from Nico, might harm the baby. Her heart was beating too fast but even when she walked more slowly, the rasp of heavy breathing grew louder.

'*Sienna, wait.*'

The commanding voice could only belong to one person. Glancing over her shoulder, she saw Nico through the mist and rain. He must have come straight from the gym and was still wearing a pair of sweatpants. As he came closer, she saw that the rain had slicked his chest hairs against his naked torso, but it was the expression on his face that made her heart turn over. Anger and something else that she dared not define sharpened his features so that he looked predatory—and it occurred to her as he ran towards her that she was the prey.

It was crazy to even try to outrun him, but she tried anyway. 'Leave me alone,' she yelled at him over her shoulder as she tore along a path that led into the ruins of an old manor house that had long since burnt down in a fire. It was here that she had made love with Nico for the first time ten years ago. Only the outer stone walls of the house remained standing, but the outhouse was still intact and partially roofed.

She gave a cry when he caught up with her. His hand landed on her shoulder and he turned her round to face him. '*I'm* not the one leaving.' He flung the words at her. 'It's you, always you who walks away. But you are not leaving me this time. I won't allow it.'

'You can't stop me.' She gasped when he scooped her up in his arms and pushed his way through the tangled weeds at the entrance to the ruined outhouse. Purple heather covered the floor and he lay them both down onto the springy carpet.

'You don't think, *cara*?' he growled, catching her wrists and holding them in one hand.

The fight drained out of her. 'Why would you want to stop me leaving?' she whispered. The hopelessness of it was unbearable.

'Because I love you.'

'Don't.' She closed her eyes to block out his handsome face so close to hers. Too close. Even now, when she was hurting so badly, she longed to press her lips to the firm line of his jaw and kiss his mouth, lose herself in the passion that would swiftly build between them. But sex without his love would destroy her because she deserved more. 'Don't say it when I know you don't meant it. I deserve your honesty at least, Nico.'

'Sienna, look at me.' Nico's voice was low, raw, *hurting* as she hurt.

Her lashes flew open and she trembled at the wealth of emotion in his eyes. His mouth twisted. 'Why don't you believe me?'

'How *can* I believe you when you told me that you don't believe in love? You only want your baby.'

'I want you. I *love* you.' He stared into her eyes, as if by force of his strong will he could convince her. 'Danny recognised what I didn't ten years ago,' he said thickly. 'He knew I was in love with you. He was jealous of me and realised he could exploit my feelings for you, so he lied and told me that you and he had been lovers.'

He smoothed her hair back from her face with an unsteady hand, and the betraying gesture made Sienna realise with a sense of shock that the emotional turmoil in his eyes was real. 'When I confronted Danny, he admitted the part he had played in breaking us up, and I don't know if I can ever forgive him,' Nico said, his voice raw.

'When our marriage broke up, I told myself I was glad.' His eyes darkened when she flinched. 'I didn't want to care too deeply, and for eight years I believed that I was invulnerable. Love was for fools.' His mouth crooked in a wry smile. 'And then I looked around the church at my brother's wedding and saw the most beautiful woman I'd ever seen, and everything I thought I knew about myself imploded. I had to have you and for a while I convinced myself that I could have an affair with you on my terms.'

'But then I fell pregnant,' Sienna said flatly, 'and it changed everything.'

He shook his head. 'No, *tesoro*. I fell in love with you and it scared the hell out of me.'

'Nico…' The glitter of moisture in his eyes shattered the last of her defences. She pulled her wrists out of his grip and laid her hand against his cheek. A tremor ran through her when he turned his head and pressed his lips against her palm. 'I love you,' she said softly. 'I always have and I always will.'

'Then why did you leave me?' It was a cry from his heart, from the twelve-year-old boy inside the man.

'I was scared too. I had been hurt before.' She struggled to speak past the lump in her throat. 'I thought that if we married and then I lost this baby too, you would regret that I was your wife.'

'Sweetheart, don't cry.' His voice shook. 'When I proposed to you and put my ring on your finger, it was because I love you with all my heart and soul. I want to spend the rest of my life with you and face whatever the future holds together.'

The truth was in his eyes when he looked deeply into hers, and it was in his kiss when he claimed her lips. He kissed her with reverence and passion and such sweet sensuality that Sienna thought she would die from the beauty of it. She curved her arms around his neck and ran her fingers through the dark silk of his hair while he deepened the kiss and passion flared like wildfire between them, setting them both ablaze.

It was wild and elemental as their need became a clamouring hunger. Desire, hot and fierce, made them both shake with anticipation as their wet clothes were hastily discarded. And then there was the delight of skin against skin, the rough hairs on his chest scraping against her soft breasts. He traced his hands over her body that was ripe now with his child. The hunger in his eyes reassured her. His need was there for her to see, thick and hard in her hands.

'I love you.' It was a vow; a plea for forgiveness and an everlasting promise. 'I don't think I can wait, *cara mia.*'

But he was patient as he made her body sing with his hands and mouth, and with his wicked tongue that drove her out of her mind when he curled it around each of her nipples before he moved lower and pushed her legs apart to bestow an intimate caress that made her cry out his name, her need. 'Now, Nico, please…'

And then he lifted himself over her and entered her slowly, waiting while she caught her breath and her internal muscles relaxed as he filled her. He made love to her with tenderness and passion, thrusting deep and taking her higher until she hovered on the edge with him and they tumbled together into the magical place that was uniquely theirs.

A long time later they walked back to the house hand in hand and apologised to Iris for missing lunch. 'A walk in the rain, half undressed.' Her brows lifted. 'I may not be as young as I was, but I recognise love when I see it. And besides, Sienna has a sprig of heather in her hair.'

'Do you think your grandmother guessed what we were doing on the moors?' Sienna muttered when she followed Nico into the bedroom.

'I'm sure she did,' he said as he drew her into his arms and slid her engagement ring back onto her finger. 'My grandmother is very astute, and I expect she'll guess what I am about to do right now.'

Sienna smiled at him, her heart in her eyes and her love for him blazing so fiercely that Nico caught his breath. 'What are you going to do?' she asked him.

'I'm going to love you for ever, *mio amore*.'

EPILOGUE

SIENNA BECAME NICO'S wife for the second time in
a simple but deeply moving ceremony in the town
hall a few miles from Villa Lionard. And on a cold,
crisp winter's day their son took everyone by surprise when he arrived earlier than expected. The
baby was four weeks early, but he was strong and
healthy, and Sienna wept tears of relief and joy. Alessandro De Conti had his parents wrapped around
one of his tiny fingers within seconds of his birth.

'Never be afraid,' Nico whispered when he cradled his son in his arms in the delivery room. 'Your
mamma and *papà* will protect you and care for you,
and most of all they will show you that love is a wonderful gift to treasure for ever.'

He looked at Sienna, his brave and beautiful wife
who had given him his son and given him so much
more besides. 'I love you and I love Alessandro,' he
said huskily, shaken by the depth of emotion he felt.
'My heart is full, *cara mia*.'

Eighteen months later...

Cotton-wool clouds dotted the forget-me-not-blue sky above St Augustine's church in Much Matcham on a perfect summer's day. Inside the church, the sun streamed through the stained-glass windows, creating colourful rainbows on the stone floor of the nave. Huge arrangements of pink roses and white lilies had been placed at the ends of each aisle and their exquisite scent pervaded the air.

Nico was standing in the front porch of the church, from where he could see the congregation who filled the pews and were waiting for the wedding blessing ceremony to begin. The two grandmothers, Iris and Rose, were at the front of the church, and sitting with them was Alessandro, being supervised by his nanny. He was a toddler now, full of mischief and adored by his parents.

Also sitting in the front pew was Danny and his heavily pregnant wife. 'You need to end the rift with your brother,' Sienna had told Nico a few weeks after Alessandro's birth. 'Family is important, and I know you miss him.'

It had taken time, but gradually Nico had forgiven Danny, and a new understanding had developed between the brothers. Danny revealed how he had felt second-best to Nico, and Nico had been more than happy to hand over the running of the Sethbury estate to his brother. Now Danny and Victoria—who he plainly adored—lived in a wing of Sethbury Hall and were awaiting the imminent birth of a daughter, a cousin for Alessandro and a third great-grandchild for Iris. Luigi of course would always be remembered as the first child of the next generation and would be for ever loved and missed by his parents, Nico acknowledged with a soft sigh. Sienna's mother and her partner had flown over from their home in Spain, and Sienna's best friend, Carley, was there. The enormous blue silk hat decorated with peacock feathers could only belong to his mother, Nico thought wryly. But there was not a chance that Jacqueline would outshine the bride.

He heard a car pull up, and when he walked out onto the front step his breath caught in his throat as he watched Sienna get out of the car. She was wearing an ivory silk and lace gown and held a bouquet of pink rosebuds. Her rich burgundy hair was swept up into an elegant chignon and she wore a sparkling tiara.

'You wait,' she'd told him when they had decided to have their wedding blessed in a church ceremony so they could share their happiness with all their friends and family. 'This is absolutely the last time that I'll be a bride and I'm going for the full works.'

Nico forced himself to wait while the woman he loved more than life itself walked gracefully up the steps and took his arm. 'You look so beautiful, you take my breath away,' he whispered as they walked together towards the altar.

And there in front of family and friends, in front of two misty-eyed grandmothers and a lively little boy who had his father's dark hair and his mother's grey eyes, Nico held his wife's hand and pressed his lips to her finger where her wedding band now sat next to the diamond eternity ring he had placed there when they had woken in each other's arms that morning.

Sienna smiled and the unguarded expression in her eyes made Nico's heart explode in his chest. 'I love you,' she said softly.

'And I love you, *tesoro*. For eternity.'

* * * * *

If you enjoyed
Reunited by a Shock Pregnancy
you're sure to enjoy these other stories
by Chantelle Shaw!

The Throne He Must Take
Hired for Romano's Pleasure
Wed for His Secret Heir
The Virgin's Sicilian Protector

Available now!

COMING NEXT MONTH FROM

H HARLEQUIN

Presents®

Available April 16, 2019

#3713 CLAIMED FOR THE SHEIKH'S SHOCK SON
Secret Heirs of Billionaires
by Carol Marinelli

For Khalid, nothing compares to the bombshell that Aubrey's had his secret child! Claiming his son is non-negotiable for this proud prince... But claiming Aubrey will prove a much more delicious challenge!

#3714 A CINDERELLA TO SECURE HIS HEIR
Cinderella Seductions
by Michelle Smart

To secure his heir, Alessio will use his incredible chemistry with his nephew's legal guardian, Beth, and command her to marry him! But will their intensely passionate marriage be enough for this innocent Cinderella?

#3715 THE ITALIAN'S TWIN CONSEQUENCES
One Night With Consequences
by Caitlin Crews

Sarina's used to working with powerful men. But she isn't prepared for the fire billionaire Matteo ignites in her! Succumbing to indescribable pleasure changes everything between them. Especially when she discovers she's pregnant—with the Italian's twins!

#3716 PREGNANT BY THE COMMANDING GREEK
by Natalie Anderson

Leon can't resist indulging in a night of pleasure with Ettie! But her pregnancy bombshell demands action. Leon's heir will not be born out of wedlock, so Ettie must say "I do"...

HPCNM0419RA

#3717 PENNILESS VIRGIN TO SICILIAN'S BRIDE
Conveniently Wed!
by Melanie Milburne

Gabriel offers a simple exchange—for her hand in marriage he'll save Francesca's ancestral home. And their attraction can only sweeten the deal. But her secret innocence is enough to make Gabriel crave his wife—forever!

#3718 WEDDING NIGHT REUNION IN GREECE
Passion in Paradise
by Annie West

When Emma overhears Christo admitting he married her for convenience, she flees, not expecting him to follow—with seduction in mind! Will a night in her husband's bed show Emma there's more than convenience to their marriage?

#3719 MARRIAGE BARGAIN WITH HIS INNOCENT
by Cathy Williams

Matias never does anything by halves. So when Georgie confesses his family believes they're engaged, he'll ensure everyone believes their charade. But discovering Georgie's true innocence suddenly makes their fake relationship feel unexpectedly—deliciously!—real...

#3720 BILLIONAIRE'S MEDITERRANEAN PROPOSAL
by Julia James

To convince everyone he's off-limits, Tara will pose as billionaire Marc's girlfriend. But when the world believes they're engaged, becoming his fiancée pushes their desire to new heights! Dare Tara believe their Mediterranean fantasy could be real?

Get 4 FREE REWARDS!

We'll send you 2 FREE Books plus <u>2</u> FREE Mystery Gifts.

Harlequin Presents® books feature a sensational and sophisticated world of international romance where sinfully tempting heroes ignite passion.

FREE
Value Over
$20

'Do not misunderstand me. Getting custody of Domenico is my primary motivation. He is a Palvetti and he deserves to take his place with us, his family. In my care he can have everything. But if custody were all I wanted, he would already be with me.'

She took another sip of her drink. Normally she hated whisky in any of its forms, but right then the burn it made in her throat was welcome. It was the fire she needed to cut through her despair. 'Then what do you want? I think of all the work we've done, all the hours spent, all the money spent—'

'I wanted to get to know you.'

She finally allowed herself to look at him. 'Why?'

The emerald eyes that had turned her veins to treacle lasered into hers. He leaned forward and spoke quietly. 'I wanted to learn about you through more than the reports and photographs my investigators provided me with.'

'You had me investigated?'

'I thought it prudent to look into the character of the person caring for my nephew.'

Her head spun so violently she felt dizzy with the motion.

He'd been spying on her.

She should have known Alessio's silence since she'd refused his offer of money in exchange for Dom had been ominous. She'd lulled herself into a false sense of security and underestimated him and underestimated the lengths he would be prepared to go to.

Everything Domenico had said about his brother was true, and more.

Through the ringing in her ears, he continued, 'Do not worry. Any childhood indiscretions are your own concern. I only wanted to know about the last five years of your life and what I learned about you intrigued me. It was clear to me from the investigators' reports and your refusal of my financial offer that you had an affection for my nephew…'

'Affection does not cover a fraction of the love I feel for him,' she told him fiercely.

'I am beginning to understand that for myself.'

'Good, because I will never let him go without a fight.'

'I understand that, too, but you must know that if it came to a fight, you would never win. I could have gone through the British courts and made my case for custody—I think we are both aware that my wealth and power would have outmatched your efforts—but Domenico is familiar with you and it is better for him if you remain in his life than be cut off.'

She held his gaze and lifted her chin. 'I'm all he knows.'

He raised a nonchalant shoulder. 'But he is very young. If it comes to it, he will adapt without you quickly. For the avoidance of doubt, I do not want that outcome.'

'What outcome do you want?'

'Marriage.'

Drumbeats joined the chorus of sound in her head. 'What on earth are you talking about?'

He rose from his seat and headed back to the bar. 'Once I have Domenico in Milan, it will be a simple matter for me to take legal guardianship of him.' He poured himself another large measure and swirled it in his glass. 'I recognise your genuine affection for each other and have no wish to separate you. In all our best interests, I am prepared to marry you.'

Dumbfounded, Beth shook her head, desperately trying to rid herself of all the noise in her ears so she could think properly. 'I wouldn't marry you if you paid me.'

Don't miss

A Cinderella to Secure His Heir.

Available May 2019 wherever
Harlequin® Presents books and ebooks are sold.

www.Harlequin.com